## "I can't be pregna

"Oh, Andrew, I can't be!

"I have no idea. I can't—" he began, and then Libby leapt to her feet, twisting her hands together, her mouth open, her breath jerking in and out of tortured lungs.

"Well, apparently you can," he said. "I can't believe I've been so *stupid!*"

"It's not your fault…."

He got to his feet and walked over to her, resting his hand gently on her shoulder. "Libby, I'm so sorry. If I'd had the merest *hint* that there was any possibility I could get you pregnant I would never have made love to you without using protection."

She shook her head. "I knew how important it was not to get pregnant with this hanging over me, but I did nothing about it. You *know* how I feel about the prospect of conceiving a child who might be—" She broke off, pressing her fists to her mouth, her eyes wild with grief and anger and despair.

He wasn't infertile. Andrew was sure he had been, but apparently not any longer. And now the woman he loved more than anyone else in the world was carrying his child.

Dear Reader,

Suffolk is a beautiful county. I've lived here for nearly thirty years—married here, raised my family here and it's become my home. Often when I'm contemplating a setting for a book, I think of Suffolk. It has a flat, high plateau, rolling countryside and little pleated valleys with winding lanes and pretty cottages, plus a beautiful coastline with river estuaries and some stunning stately homes. About the only thing it doesn't have are hills, but I can forgive it that for all the other things.

In this book, I gave my hero a family home right here in Suffolk near the coast, in a wooded river valley. It's a beautiful old home steeped in tradition, with aristocratic connections and responsibilities. Motivated by his brother who had overcome a life-threatening condition as a child, Andrew has dedicated his life and career to helping children. He is also a man who longs for normality—a wife and family—so I gave him Libby, a woman for whom the dream of family may only ever be just that.

My characters' ensuing heartache is sadly something many people can relate to, and I found it heart-wrenching to write. Luckily, I was able to give Andrew and Libby their happy ending. But I never lost sight of the fact that for many couples in a similar position, that happy ending won't come true. Think of them, as you read my story, and thank your stars for what you have. I do, every day.

With love,

*Caroline*

# THE SURGEON'S MIRACLE

## Caroline Anderson

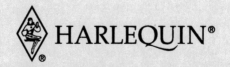

### HARLEQUIN®

TORONTO • NEW YORK • LONDON
AMSTERDAM • PARIS • SYDNEY • HAMBURG
STOCKHOLM • ATHENS • TOKYO • MILAN • MADRID
PRAGUE • WARSAW • BUDAPEST • AUCKLAND

Recycling programs
for this product may
not exist in your area.

ISBN-13: 978-0-373-06735-0

THE SURGEON'S MIRACLE

First North American Publication 2010.

# THE SURGEON'S MIRACLE

# CHAPTER ONE

'Got a minute, Libby?'

'Sure—' She looked up and flashed him a harassed smile, but it faded as soon as she caught sight of him. 'Wow, you look rough. I heard you were busy—sounds like a grim night.'

He grunted. If he looked half as rough as he felt, he must look like hell, because grim wasn't the word. 'It was pretty dire. There were three of us in there—someone removing a blood clot from his brain while I stabilised his fractures and someone else sorted out his spleen. It was pretty touch and go for a while,' he agreed. 'We were in Theatre for hours. The kid's only seven—it was a hit and run.'

Libby winced sympathetically. 'Poor little mite. How could anybody do that?'

'Search me. I have no idea.'

'How's he doing?'

He lifted his shoulders—in truth, there wasn't much he could add. 'He's stable—sort of.' That was enough. The bare bones—all he had the energy to explain.

Libby nodded, then bit her lip. 'Can you give me a sec, Andrew? I won't be long, I just need to finish this off.'

'That's fine, you carry on, I'm not in a hurry,' he murmured.

He wasn't. He'd given little Jacob the full focus of his energy and concentration, and it was time to step back and centre himself again. The neuro had got the clot out, the GS had glued the liver and removed the spleen and he'd restored the circulation to his feet and stabilised his legs and pelvis with external fixators, and somehow Jacob had turned the corner and was now in the paediatric intensive care unit, heavily sedated and hopefully on the road to recovery.

He'd just checked on the little boy again, and he was improving slightly, and although it was far too soon to be overconfident, for now, at least, Andrew could relax.

Goodness knows, he needed to. He was exhausted, in sore need of a break, and there was nothing more he could do anyway, for now, except watch Libby, and that was fine. He was more than happy to lounge against the doorjamb and watch the pretty young ward sister finish her task while his mind free-wheeled.

Ideally he'd be at home in bed after a night like that, but life wasn't ideal, and although it was only seven-thirty he'd already spent half an hour with Jacob's parents this morning, to fill them in on his part in the proceedings—and in thirty-six hours, after another full day at work, he'd have to go home and face the weekend from hell—another excuse for his mother to trot out a whole load of single girls in the vain hope that he'd find one to settle down with and secure the future of the family line.

It didn't make any difference that his brother's wife was pregnant. If anything it made it worse, because it just made his single status all the more obvious—and his mother, ever the fixer, wanted him to be as happy as Will. So the girls would all be there, and he'd have to deal with them all, from his hopelessly infatuated cousin Charlotte to the predatory gold-diggers, via the perfectly nice girls that he just wasn't interested in, and watching it all unfold would be his beloved mother with that hopeful look on her face.

Oh, hell. He was too tired for this, sick of warding them off, sick of making excuses to his mother, and the last thing—absolutely the *last* thing—he needed was this party. Correction—parties. Two of them.

With a muffled groan, he shifted his shoulders against the doorframe and watched Libby thoughtfully as she entered notes onto the computer at her desk. Nice girl, he thought. Really nice girl. If things were different, he might be tempted, but they weren't. More's the pity, because she really was lovely in every way.

Her lip was caught between even, perfect white teeth, her long lashes dark crescents against her creamy cheeks as she looked down at the keyboard. A lock of rich brown hair slid down out of her ponytail and she tucked it absently behind her ear. It looked soft, glossy, as if she'd just washed it this morning—in which case it would smell of apples. It always smelled of apples when she'd washed it…

How had he registered that? Goodness knows. Not deliberately, any more than he'd deliberately noticed the freckles scattered over her nose, or the curve of her bottom as she bent over a child, or the fact that even the hideously unflattering tunic couldn't disguise her perfectly proportioned breasts.

He wondered what she was doing this weekend. Something normal, he'd bet. The washing, or going to the cinema with friends. Curling up with a good book on the sofa next to her boyfriend.

He frowned. Scrub that last image. Although he'd never heard her talk about a boyfriend, he thought, his mind ticking over. And if all she *was* going to be doing was pottering about at home—

'Doing anything exciting this weekend?' he found himself saying before he could stop himself, and then held his breath for her reply.

Libby looked up from the notes she was finishing off and leant back in her chair, finally allowing herself the luxury of looking at him again. He looked exhausted—exhausted and rumpled and sexy, even more so than usual, so she took her time, enjoying the view.

'Now, then, let me think,' she said with a teasing smile. 'Flying to Paris, dinner in a fabulous restaurant, then going to the top of the Eiffel Tower to see the lights, strolling along the Seine by moonlight—or then again, maybe I'll just stay at home and tackle my laundry basket before it suffers a fatal rupture, and then get the duster out of retirement.'

He chuckled and shrugged away from the doorframe, with a lazy, economical gesture that did odd things to her pulse rate, and sauntered over, propping his taut, firm buttocks on the edge of her desk, folding his arms and staring down at her thoughtfully, long legs crossed at the ankle.

He'd had a hellish night, but he still managed to look drop-dead gorgeous. He was wearing theatre scrubs, drab and sexless and unrevealing, but on him they just looked amazing. He was so close she could feel his warmth, smell the subtle, masculine fragrance of his skin. If she moved her hand just a fraction to the right—

'Just your own laundry?'

'Well, I don't take in washing to supplement my income, if that's what you're implying!' she joked, convinced that it couldn't possibly be a corny chat-up line. Not from Andrew.

He grinned wearily. 'God forbid! Actually, I was trying in my rather clumsy and unsubtle way to find out if you live alone.'

Good heavens. So it *was* a chat-up line? Surely not. She didn't get that lucky—did she? She felt her mouth go dry and her heart hitch in her chest before she talked herself out of believing it, and then she couldn't resist the urge to poke a little fun at herself. 'Actually, no,' she said, pausing, then went on, 'but the cat doesn't generate a lot of washing—and before you say it,' she added quickly as he started to chuckle, 'I know that makes me a sad old spinster, but I love my cat and she's good company—even if she does shed all over my clothes and wake me up in the night for food. And—no, there's nobody else if that's what you were asking, either live-in or otherwise.'

One side of his mouth kicked up a fraction more. 'In which case, if the cat doesn't mind, I don't suppose I can persuade you to put the laundry on hold and come away with me to the country for the weekend? I can't promise you the Eiffel Tower, but we can certainly stroll by a river and I can guarantee the food will be good.'

Her heart lurched again and she sucked in a quiet breath and saved the file on the computer, then swivelled the chair round and made herself look calmly up at him, convinced she'd misheard. Either that or gone mad. But he'd wanted to talk to her, so maybe—

'Run that by me again? Did I imagine it, or did I just hear what sounded like an invitation for a dirty weekend?'

He gave another soft chuckle, then pulled a face and rubbed his jaw with his hand. Goodness knows when he'd shaved. Not that morning, anyway, and she heard the tantalising rasp of stubble against his fingers and nearly whimpered.

'Tempting thought,' he said, 'but no. I have—' He broke off and let out his breath on a gusty laugh that was half-sigh. 'It's my mother's sixtieth birthday party, and I can't get out of it. She's having a house party and a ball and the whole shebang, and I just know that all the single women she knows of childbearing age and the seventh cousin eight times removed will be dragged out of the woodwork and paraded in front of me—again. And there's nothing wrong with any of them, but—you know, if I wanted to have a relationship with any of them, I would have done it by now, but I don't, and I'm too tired for it, Libby,' he said with a sigh, scrubbing his hand round the back of his neck. 'I've been up all night, I'm going to have damn all time to take it easy before tomorrow night when it all kicks off and I really can't be bothered with making endless small talk and then because I haven't been downright rude, having to find excuses for not meeting up for coffee or going for drinks or having dinner or going to the races.'

'So,' she said slowly, torn between pity because he was so tired, wondering how big his ego really was, and trying not to drool too badly as he flexed his shoulders again, 'you want me as—let me get this right—some kind of deflector to shield you from this rampant horde of women that most men would give their eye teeth for a crack at?'

He chuckled softly, the sound rippling through her and turning her to jelly. 'Hardly a rampant horde, but, yes, if you like,' he said with a grin. 'But mostly I need someone to deflect my mother's attention from my single status—which incidentally I have no intention of changing in a hurry, much to her great disappointment.'

He was single? Amazing. How? And more to the point, why? What a tragic waste!

He tipped his head on one side, rolling his shoulders again as if he was easing out the kinks. 'So—will you?'

'Will I—?' she asked, distracted by those shoulders,

her fingers itching to dig into the taut muscles and ease away the tension she knew she'd find there.

'Be my deflector? Let me drag you away from the laundry basket and the duster and take you away with me to the country for a strictly no-strings weekend?'

Her heart hiccuped at the thought, and she sat back and looked up into his eyes. His piercing, ice-blue eyes with the navy rims round the irises and the fetching, sexy little crinkles in the outer corners. Eyes that even bloodshot with exhaustion could turn her legs to spaghetti and her brains to mush with a single glance.

'So what's in it for me?' she asked bluntly, knowing in advance what her answer would be and how with the best will in the world she didn't have it in her to turn down an invitation from the most gorgeous man she'd ever met in her life—even if she didn't stand a chance, even if she was beating her head against a brick wall and getting that close to a work colleague ever again was top of her list of taboos.

He shrugged, wondering how he could sell it to her, suddenly desperate for her company, for her to say yes. 'A fabulous dinner tomorrow night, a lazy weekend in the beautiful Suffolk countryside, peaceful walks by the river with the dogs, a glittering formal ball on Saturday night.'

'Good food, you said?'

She was hooked. Andrew smiled and felt his heart thud with what had to be relief. 'Good food, good wine—good company…'

'Yours, I take it—not that you're vain or anything,' she said, her voice rich with mockery, and he chuckled and straightened up, refusing to be insulted. Actually he was refreshed by her blunt straightforwardness and teasing good-humour, and, oddly, incredibly fascinated by the tiny spangles of gold in the depths of her extraordinary sea-green eyes.

'Absolutely not. But I have it on good authority that I can be a charming companion, I can dance without treading on your toes—and unlike your cat, I won't moult on your clothes or demand food in the middle of the night. I'm even housetrained.'

She smiled, but her eyes were searching. 'No strings, you said?'

He felt a tug of disappointment and dismissed it. 'With the great and the good of Suffolk chaperoning us? Not a chance. Just you, me, and every single woman in a hundred miles.'

'And good food.'

'And good food. Excellent food. Mum uses a brilliant caterer for these functions.'

She nodded thoughtfully. 'So—this weekend. How dressy is it?'

He thought of the women who'd inevitably be there in their designer originals, and pulled a face. Libby probably didn't have anything like that, not on a nurse's salary. 'Dressy. Black tie tomorrow for dinner, white tie on Saturday for the ball.'

Libby's eyes widened. 'Wow. That's pretty formal. Tailcoats and floor-length gowns, isn't it?'

He nodded, studying her thoughtfully, hoping she wouldn't use it as an excuse to turn him down—or that she'd come and be embarrassed by the other women. He'd hate that for her.

'Right,' she said, after a short, considering pause.

Right, what? Right, she'd come, or right, it sounded like a nightmare and she wouldn't be seen dead near the place? 'Is that a problem? Do you have anything suitable?'

'I'm sure I can dredge up the odd rag,' she said drily,

and he felt some of the tension ease out of him as she went on, 'So where will we stay?'

'At the house,' he said without hesitation. 'I'll tell my mother I'm bringing you. She'll be delighted.' Ridiculously delighted.

'Does she even know who I am?'

He felt his mouth twitch. 'No. I've never mentioned you. Or anyone else, come to that, so you're safe. You can be as inventive as you like, so long as you let me in on it.'

Libby sighed and rolled her eyes. 'Don't you go spinning your mother porkies, now, Andrew, or I won't come. We work together, you've asked me up for the weekend. End of. No inventiveness. I don't want to spend the entire weekend like a moonstruck teenager pretending to be in love with you.'

He was tempted to ask if it would be such a hardship, but thought better of it at the last second and smiled reassuringly. 'Of course not. I'll just tell her I'm bringing a plus one. I'll let her make any further leaps herself. Don't worry, you won't have to pretend to smile while I grope you for effect.'

Pity, she thought, but managed what she hoped was a normal smile. 'So—what time does this extravaganza start?'

'Seven for seven-thirty. I'd like to leave at six, but Murphy's Law says it's unlikely. Is that OK?'

'Fine,' she said, not sure if she'd lost her marbles or won the lottery.

'Great. I'll see you later.'

Lottery, she decided, watching him walk away. Good food, good wine—and definitely good company. And it might answer some of her abundant questions about the most enigmatic and attractive man she'd met in her entire twenty-seven years...

* * *

'You're doing *what*?'

'Going home with him for the weekend. It's his mother's sixtieth birthday party and there's a ball.'

'Good God,' Amy said weakly, and stared at her open-mouthed.

'What?'

'What? *What?* You stun me. You must be the only single woman in Suffolk who wouldn't kill for an invitation like that.'

She shook her head quickly, resisting the urge to tell Amy that according to Andrew all the single women in Suffolk had already been invited. 'No. It's not an invitation *like that*. It's strictly no strings.'

Amy laughed till the tears ran down her face. 'Yeah, right! You're going home for the weekend with *that man* and you're saying it's no strings? Are you both dead, or what? And what on earth are you going to wear?'

She felt a flicker of unease. 'I don't know. Clothes?' she said helpfully, and the physio rolled her eyes.

'Dear heaven. You do realise who'll be there, don't you? I mean, this isn't your ordinary, everyday birthday party for a little old lady.'

'She's only sixty!'

'She's only *Lady Ashenden*!' Amy said, imitating her voice, and Libby felt her own jaw drop. She snatched it back up and tried not to hyperventilate.

'Lady Ashenden—as in, Ashenden Place? The one that's open to the public? No! No, his name's not Ashenden, don't be silly!'

'No, he's the Hon. Andrew Langham-Jones, first son of Lord and Lady Ashenden, heir to the Ashenden estate, which as you rightly say is open to the public and only one of the most beautiful country piles in Suffolk—not to mention the family coffers and the flipping title! He's one of the most eligible bachelors around—good grief, Libby, I can't believe you didn't know about him!'

'Maybe because I don't gossip?' she suggested mildly, wondering if she ought to take it up if she was going to accept random invitations from gorgeous men without re-alising what she was letting herself in for. And of course, if he was the future Lord Ashenden, no wonder all the dowagers were trotting their daughters out! He wasn't being vain or egotistical at all, he was just being realistic, and she couldn't believe she'd been so stupid—but Amy could. Oh, yes. And Amy said so. Bluntly.

'You don't need to gossip, you just need to be alive! You just—you live in a cocoon, do you know that? You go home every night to your little house and your little cat and you snuggle down in front of the television and *you have no idea what's going on right under your nose!* No wonder you're still single!'

'I'm happy being single,' she lied, trying not to think about the lonely nights and the long weekends and the ri-diculous farce of speed dating and internet dating and blind dates that she'd given up on ages ago.

'Rubbish,' Amy said briskly, and eyed her up and down. 'So—what are you wearing for this event?'

'Two events,' she corrected, wincing inwardly when she thought about it. *Lady Ashenden?* Oh, rats. 'A black-tie dinner tomorrow night and a white-tie formal ball the fol-lowing night.'

Amy's eyes widened, then narrowed critically as she studied her friend, making Libby feel like an insect skewered on a pin. 'It's a pity your boobs are so lush,' Amy said candidly. 'I've got a fabulous ballgown—that smoky bluey-green one. But you'll probably fall out of it. Still, you can try it. It's the only long one I've got that's suitable and it's cut on the cross so it'll drape nicely and it'll be brilliant with your eyes. And you've got your classic LBD for tomorrow, haven't you?'

'If it doesn't need cleaning. I expect the cat's been sleeping on it—joke!' she added hastily, as Amy opened her mouth to tell her off again. 'It'll be fine. I had it cleaned after Christmas. And I've got a fairly decent pair of heels that do nice things to my legs.'

'They don't need to. You've got fabulous legs—well, you did have, the last time you let them out into the fresh air, which was ages ago, but I don't suppose they've changed. What time does your shift finish?'

'Three, but I've got to go home and feed the cat and put the washing on or I won't have anything at all to wear for the weekend.'

'Right, I'm off at five, so that gives you two hours and then I want you round at mine and we'll go through my wardrobe and see what I've got, because I know you haven't got anything unless you've got a secret life I don't know about. I can't remember the last time you told me about a date, and apart from this dreadful uniform the only other thing I ever see you in is jeans. Never mind, we'll find something even if I have to send you out shopping tomorrow. Actually, on second thoughts *I'll* go shopping. I can't trust you to buy anything sensible.'

Sensible? Libby nearly laughed out loud. She couldn't imagine that what Amy had in mind for her was in any way *sensible*, but she didn't have many options and she had even less time. 'I'm sure the bluey-green one will be fine,' she said with more confidence than she felt. 'I'll wear a minimiser bra.'

Amy laughed again as if she'd said something hysterically funny. 'Yeah, right. Just try the dress first and then we'll worry about the underwear. OK, I'm done here on the ward, I'm going back down to the gym to do my outpatients' list, and in between I'll be thinking about your outfits for the weekend. I might have another dress that would do if that one doesn't fit. I'll see you later—and don't forget to come round. I'll feed you. Half-five—and not a minute later. And bring your shoes and the LBD. Oh, and your jewellery and some bras.'

'Yeah, yeah—you are the most atrocious nag.'

'You'll love me this weekend when you don't look silly.'

'I hope so,' she muttered under her breath, and tugging her quote, dreadful, unquote uniform straight, she went to find Lucas, a fourteen-year-old who'd nearly lost his foot a week ago after a stupid stunt on his bike had gone horribly wrong. Andrew had realigned all the bones using an external fixator, but the surgery had been complicated, his recovery was going to be slow and Lucas was impatient.

He'd just gone for a walk with his mother, using his crutches, and he'd been gone longer than she liked. It was his first excursion from the ward, the first time he'd been off without supervision from a member of staff; Amy had thought the exercise would do him good, but he'd missed his lunch now and Libby was getting concerned.

She found him in the corridor, propped up on a window sill and looking pale and shaky, and she smiled and perched next to him, wondering where his mother was. Poor woman. She was trying to juggle the family and be there for Lucas, but it wasn't easy for any of the mothers, and sometimes something had to give.

'Hi, Lucas. You've been gone a while—everything OK?'

The lanky teenager shrugged. 'S'pose. Mum had to take Kyle to the doctor. My nan rang—he's sick.'

'Oh, dear, that's a shame. Look, your lunch is waiting. Why don't I fetch a chair and you can ride back to the ward? You've probably done enough for the first time.'

'I can do it myself,' he insisted, shrugging up off the window sill and wobbling slightly on the crutches. Libby frowned. He had to learn how to use them, but the last thing he needed was to go over and damage the leg again, and he was strictly non-weight-bearing at the moment.

She fell into step beside him. 'OK, if you're sure. I'll walk back with you—it's a good excuse to have a break, and I could do with some time out. You guys are wearing me down!'

He grinned and took a few steps, but he had to pause again on the way, leaning over on the crutches and getting his breath, and Libby heard a quiet footfall behind her.

'How's it going, Lucas?'

She didn't need to turn to know who it was, and her pulse picked up as she turned to him with a smile. 'He's doing really well.'

Andrew grinned at him. 'Good man.'

Lucas straightened up again, Andrew's praise having a visible effect on his mood. He was tall—a good head taller than Libby, but for all his youth he could look Andrew in the eye already, and he had a way to go before he finished growing.

'I think this is the first time I've seen you standing up—you're going to be seriously tall, aren't you?' Andrew said, eyeing him thoughtfully, and Lucas shrugged.

'Always was. I'm going to be a basketball player.' His words tailed off, his face crumpling, but Andrew wouldn't let it go.

'Give it time,' he said softly. 'You can still do that. Your leg will heal.'

'Are you sure? 'Cos it doesn't feel any better yet. It's gonna take for *ever* and I feel like about a hundred.'

'Lucas, it's only been just over a week,' he said gently. 'It'll take a while, but I've fixed all the bones together, and once they've all knitted back into place and we can get the hardware off your ankle, you'll soon be up and running. Just be patient. You'll get there and you'll soon get your fitness back.' He looked around. 'So where's Mum today?'

'At the doctor's with my brother. He's got tonsillitis. He gets it all the time.'

'Poor kid. I used to get tonsillitis. It's nasty.'

'Better than smashing your leg up.'

Andrew grinned wryly. 'Yeah, it probably is.' His eyes flicked to Libby's. 'I'm on my way down to A and E—lad with a classic fib fracture, apparently. I'm probably going to have to take him to Theatre, so you'll need to find room for him, but I'll be back up after I've seen him to check last night's admissions. And maybe we can find time for a coffee—I was hoping to get one earlier while we went through the notes together, but we got a little sidetracked,' he added softly, and she felt colour brush her cheeks.

So that was what he'd wanted. Not to ask her to go away for the weekend at all, but to talk through the notes. So why had he? 'I'll make you one when you get back,' she suggested, but he shook his head.

'Don't worry, I'll get them and grab some sandwiches and we can eat while we talk—unless you have plans for lunch?'

She shook her head, a wry smile tugging at her mouth. 'No. I hardly ever have time to eat, never mind plan it!'

He tutted. 'I'll get some for you, too, then, and I'll see you in a bit. It looks like you've got your hands pretty full with this young man for a minute.' He turned back to him and gave the boy's shoulder an encouraging squeeze. 'Chin up, Lucas. You'll get there.'

And with a smile at him and a slow, lazy wink at Libby, he strode off down the corridor, leaving her wondering how she was going to get through the weekend without melting into a puddle of mush.

'Right—let's get you back on the ward,' she said to Lucas, dragging her thoughts back in line, 'and you can start planning your return to basketball.'

He set off again, but by the time they got back to the ward he was exhausted, and once back at his bed she brought him his lunch and settled the rest of the boys in his bay down for a rest until the visitors arrived at three.

It took bribery and a little coercion, but finally by one-thirty they were all quiet and she headed back to the office where the endless paperwork was still waiting for her.

The paperwork, and Andrew, with sandwiches and coffee. 'I was about to start without you. Egg and cress or chicken salad?'

'Either,' she said, wondering why her office suddenly seemed so small and airless. Andrew was ripping open the packets, handing her one of each with a raised eyebrow, and she took them with a smile and tried to remember how to breathe. 'Thanks. So how's the kid with the fib fracture?'

'Sore and feeling a bit silly. Apparently the idea was to jump off his trampoline onto his skateboard, only he fell off the edge of the board when he landed.'

'Idiot! Of course he did! What *is* it with boys?'

Andrew winced. 'Don't. I can't tell you how many close shaves I had as a child. The kid's father was funny, though—reminded me of mine. He described it as an ill-conceived idea, poorly executed,' he said with a chuckle.

'Oh, dear. So no sympathy from that quarter, then,' she said, joining in his laughter while she studied the smudges under his eyes and wondered how he kept going.

'Not much. He's managed to snap the fibula but it's a nice clean break and it'll screw back easily—better than a ligament injury long term anyway. He'll be up on the ward in a minute, but he'd just had something to eat so I can't take him to Theatre till later. His name's Michael Warner,' he added, sinking his teeth into his sandwich and nearly making her whimper again.

Good grief, he was so physical! If watching him eat was going to do this to her, how on earth was she going to get through two formal dinners without disgracing herself? She dragged her eyes away and tried to be practical. 'Right. Where do you want him? On the ward with the other boys?'

'Oh, yes, put him with the lads. He's twelve, he'll fit right in—and a bit more company might stop Lucas feeling sorry for himself.'

He attacked the sandwich again, and she gave a slightly strained laugh. 'I doubt it. He's sore and cross with himself and until he's running around again like before, he'll be wallowing in self-pity and grumpy as a grumpy thing.'

They shared a smile, and her lungs stopped working for a moment, a warm, fuzzy feeling spreading through her and leaving her weak. He'd shaved at some point, and changed into trousers with a cut to die for and a shirt so soft she just ached to touch it. Or was it the man inside?

'Damn—may I?' he asked, glancing at his squalling pager, and she nodded. He spoke briefly, then sighed and put the phone down.

'Right, I have to get on. Jacob needs a look,' he said, draining his coffee and putting the paper cup in the bin. 'I've checked my patients, they all seem fine unless you know different?' She shook her head and he nodded brisk-ly. 'OK. I'll see you later. Tell young Michael I'll come. I'll stick him on the end of my afternoon list, but I'll be round before then to have a chat with him.'

'OK. Thanks for the lunch. What do I owe you?'

He gave her a lazy smile. 'Nothing. You can get them next time.'

Next time?

He headed off to PICU, and she followed him out of the office, pulling herself together and trying not to think about next time. She was having enough trouble dealing with this time!

She went into the boys' bay to sort the bed out, and stood there for a moment considering the situation. There were six of them—Lucas, and Rajesh, another boy of the same age who'd had an open fracture of his right forearm which had been fixed and plated that morning. He wouldn't be there long. Then there was Joel, a boy of fifteen who'd fallen through the roof of the conservatory climbing out of the window above when he'd been grounded; he'd suffered multiple fractures and so was now well and truly grounded until the casts on both arms and the halo frame stabilising his neck could be removed.

Then there were Christopher and Jonathan, twin broth-ers who'd fallen out of a tree when a branch had snapped, and broken three legs and one arm between them. She'd like to keep them together for company. And Nico, with repaired ligaments in his ankle. He'd been cleared for dis-charge and was waiting to go, so she moved him into a chair to wait for his parents, and as she and the health care assistant finished remaking the bed, Michael arrived in a wheelchair with his long-suffering and patient father.

'Hi, there,' she said, going out and introducing herself

with a smile. 'I'm Libby Tate, the ward sister, and you must be Michael. We're expecting you. Come on through, I'll show you to your bed.'

She'd put him between Lucas and Joel, the boy who'd fallen through the conservatory roof, and by the time he was settled against the pillows the banter had started. Good. He'd be fine, and a welcome distraction for Lucas and Joel.

She put the clipboard with his charts on the end of the bed and smiled at the boy and his father. 'Right, I'm off duty now, Michael, but the anaesthetist will be round to see you soon and Mr Langham-Jones is taking you down to Theatre in a while—he'll be up to see you afterwards to tell you how it went, and I'll be on in the morning so I'll catch up with you then. The others will look after you, won't you, boys?' she said to them all with a smile, and as soon as she'd handed over, she grabbed her coat and went out to her car, wondering if it was her imagination or if there was a spring in her step that hadn't been there earlier.

Yup. Definite spring, and she felt ridiculously light-hearted. Silly. It was a no-strings, pretend date. Not really a date at all. Her heart really shouldn't be getting excited.

But it was…

# CHAPTER TWO

THE dress was gorgeous, shot with navy and olive green so it looked like the sea on a stormy day, the colours changing as the light caught it, and by the time Amy had poured her into the dress, hitched up the front a little for decency and scooped her hair into a knot and put a necklace round her throat, no amount of reasoning with her pulse was going to make a blind bit of difference.

Amy stood back and stared at her, and shook her head slowly. 'Wow.'

'D'you think?' Libby hitched the front up again and had her hand slapped for her pains.

'Leave it. You've got gorgeous boobs, be proud of them. Stick them out and hold your head up—that's better. Fabulous. You'll knock them all dead.'

'Knock them out, more like,' she said, shuffling her bra—clearly no room for a minimiser in there with that neckline!—and biting her lip. 'Are you sure it's all right?'

But Amy just rolled her eyes and draped an exquisite oyster-pink silk and cashmere pashmina around her shoulders. 'There. You can always cover your cleavage with this if it worries you. Don't lose it, it cost a fortune and it's my only real extravagance. And you can wear it tomorrow with the black. Let me see you in it?'

So Libby changed into her dearly loved and classic little black dress, the high scoop neck and on-the-knee hemline much more demure and discreet. The back dipped to a V just above her bra strap, and there was a tiny kick-pleat at the back to allow for movement, and she loved it. It was elegant, sophisticated and timeless—which was just as well because she'd had it for three years now and by her reckoning it still owed her a substantial amount of money. It was, however, a little more snug than it had been before Christmas, and she sucked in her stomach and sighed.

'You've given me too much to eat,' she said. 'Or I have, for weeks and weeks. It's too tight.'

'It's lovely,' Amy said, standing back and eyeing her critically. 'Very demure. Very sexy.'

'It's not meant to be sexy,' she said, her eyes widening. 'It's meant to be respectable!'

'It's perfectly respectable.'

She gave up, not entirely reassured, but her time and her options were dwindling by the minute. 'Good. Can I go now? I've got to get my jeans dry somehow so I can pack them in the morning. Apparently we're leaving at six and I don't finish work till five tomorrow, so I've got to wash my hair and pack tonight—all except for the things still in the washing machine. Oh, why aren't I better organised? I really wanted my nice cream jumper but it won't be dry, it takes ages.'

'I've got a jumper you can borrow,' Amy said, rummaging in her chest of drawers and pulling out a couple of clingy little scraps.

'It's only just April! I meant a *jumper*, Amy, not a second skin!'

'You'll be fine. Here. Take them anyway, they'll suit you. You can always wear your coat if you're cold.'

'In the house?'

'They're bound to have heating, you'll be fine. Go on, scoot. You've got things to do and you need a good night's sleep or you'll have bags under your eyes.'

Not a chance, she thought. There was no way she'd sleep. She was getting ridiculously excited, and when she walked onto the ward the next morning Andrew was there, lounging against the nursing station and chatting to Lucas's parents. He looked up and met her eyes and smiled, and her heart turned over in her chest.

*Ridiculously* excited, she told herself, trying not to grin like an idiot, and she went to find the staff nurse to do handover and made a futile attempt to ignore his presence.

Andrew watched her turn away and busy herself, and resisted the temptation to cut the conversation short. Despite their encouragement and constant support of Lucas, his parents were naturally worried about their son, and he took the time to reassure them yet again before he gave in to the need to speak to Libby.

She was at the nurses' station in the middle, talking to the staff nurse who'd been on since seven, and as he excused himself and crossed over to her she looked up, her smile lighting up her face and warming him like sunshine. He propped his arms on the counter and smiled back at her, glad it was between them because he was having trouble resisting the unexpected urge to drag her into his arms and kiss her.

Not a good move. He cleared his throat slightly.

'Hi, there.'

'Hi. How's things?' she asked, her voice music to his ears. 'I hear Jacob's improving. How did you get on with Michael?'

'OK. It was absolutely straightforward. He can go home today once the physio's got him up on crutches. I'll see him in the fracture clinic next week for follow-up, but he should be fine. He was lucky.'

'He was an idiot,' she reminded him drily, and he chuckled.

'True. And Jacob's looking good, considering, so I should be able to get away reasonably promptly tonight. Are you all set?' he added softly as the staff nurse turned away to answer the phone.

'I am. All packed and ready. I washed my hair last night so I should be OK for six. Well, except that I haven't got your mother a birthday present yet.'

'You don't have to do that! Just give her a card. She'll be overwhelmed with presents and it's the last thing she'd expect.'

'Sure?'

'I'm sure. Anyway, we need to head off as soon as we can. Will you have time to get ready?'

'I should. Do you want me to change before we go, then, or are we changing there?'

'Change before we go,' he advised, trying not to sniff for the scent of apples in her hair. 'The place'll be in chaos and it'll be easier. Tell me your address and I'll pick you up as soon after six as I can get to you.'

'Fourteen Elm Grove,' she said. 'It's off Wood Farm Drive, but it's sort of buried. I can give you directions.'

'No, I'll find it. Postcode?' he asked, keying the information into his BlackBerry, and she gave him the code. 'OK. The sat-nav should do it, but you'd better give me your phone number in case it fails. It has been known.'

'Surely not,' she said with a teasing smile, and he felt a kick in his gut.

No strings? Who was he kidding?

It was going to be an interesting weekend…

The day was chaos.

After she'd seen Michael and his parents to discuss his

discharge, there were several other post-op patients who needed her attention, and of course there was Lucas. He was desperate to show off his new-found skills with the crutches, and as Amy had been up to the ward to equip Michael with his own set and show him how to use them, they were busy competing, the accident clearly not having slowed Michael down at all.

She stopped them before there was another accident, threatened to confiscate the crutches from Lucas, saw Michael off with his paperwork, then had to deal with an IV crisis in a tearful, wriggling three-year-old, and by the time she'd handed over and got away, it was nearly five-thirty. So much for her plans to slip off early!

She raced home, ripped off her uniform and had the quickest shower on record, skimmed the lightest of make-up onto her face, brushed her hair and pulled on her dress as the doorbell rang just after six. She wriggled the zip up and then, grabbing her shoes and evening bag, she ran downstairs and threw open the door, hardly pausing to greet him as she ran back into the living room, hopping on one foot as she put her shoes on on the move.

'Sorry, I'm on the drag, I couldn't get away,' she said breathlessly over her shoulder, then turned and stopped talking, because he was standing there behind her, looking utterly, devastatingly gorgeous in his DJ, the dress shirt with its immaculate black bow-tie blinding white against his skin, his jaw freshly shaved, his hair—damp?

'Either you have far too much gel in your hair or it's still wet,' she pointed out unnecessarily, and he gave a soft grunt of laughter.

'I showered and changed at the hospital or I wouldn't be here now,' he said wryly. 'I was hoping to get away early, but you know what it's like. Are you all packed and ready?'

She laughed with him. 'Sort of. Hang on.' She rummaged in her case, came up with the perfume and spritzed herself lightly, then threw it back into the case and zipped the lid. 'Now I'm ready,' she said with a slightly nervous grin. 'Will I do, or will I disgrace you?'

She gave a self-conscious twirl, and he ran his eyes over her. 'No, you won't disgrace me,' he said softly with an odd note in his voice. 'Turn around, your zip's not quite up.' And she felt his fingers cool against her heated skin as he pulled the zip up the last half-inch and fastened the hook, then smoothed it with his hand and stepped back.

'All done,' he said, and she tugged it straight and turned to pick up her coat.

'Oh, Kitty!' she wailed. 'You rascal—you can see why I wear black,' she added drily to Andrew, and he chuckled, eased the black cat off her coat, gave it a shake to remove the hair and held it out for her, settling it solicitously on her shoulders, and she wondered if she'd imagined his hands lingering for the tiniest moment.

Her shoulders tingling, she reached for her case, but he was there first, leaving her to scoop up her handbag and keys, then she followed him out of the door.

'So who feeds the cat while you're away?' he asked, opening the car door for her and tucking her coat in.

'Oh, I've got an automatic thingie. I've set it.'

'In which minute?' he asked with a chuckle, then slid behind the wheel and threw her a smile. 'You look lovely, by the way,' he added softly, making her heart hiccup and her insides tighten with anticipation. 'Much better than the uniform.'

'Well, that wouldn't be hard. It's a bit tight, though. I haven't worn it since before Christmas—I must have been staving off the cold a bit too enthusiastically,' she said with a rueful smile, but he shook his head.

'It's perfect. You look very convincing.'

Convincing. Of course. That was what this was all about, and she'd better not forget it. He'd only invited her as an afterthought, and she needed to keep that in mind. This was not, repeat not, a date. She was there to be convincing, and so convincing she'd be. End of. She flashed him a bright smile. 'Well, that's a relief! I won't be pitched out on my ear as a fraud, at least.'

They shared the smile as he started the engine and headed out into the countryside. She had no idea where they were going. Somewhere near Southwold? She'd meant to look it up on the internet to see if she could find the address of the Ashenden pile, as Amy called it, but she simply hadn't had time. She hadn't had time to draw breath, really, since yesterday morning, and as she sank back into the soft but supportive leather seat, she realised just how tired she was.

'All right?'

'Yes—it's just been a busy day. Well, busy week, really. I'm glad it's a sit-down formal dinner, because I don't think my feet would cope with standing up all evening in these ridiculous heels after a day like today.'

He peered across at the footwell in the dark. 'Are they ridiculous? I thought they looked rather good.'

He did? 'Thank you—but looking good and feeling good aren't the same thing,' she explained ruefully, and his lips twitched.

'No, I can imagine. I've only worn high heels once, and it was excruciating.'

She shifted in the seat, turning to face him, struggling to hold down her incredulous laughter. 'You've worn high heels?'

He grinned. 'And a dress. It's amazing what my brother can persuade me to do for charity,' he said drily.

That piqued her interest—that and the thought of Andrew in a dress and heels. 'Any particular one?'

'Meningococcal disease. He had it as a teenager and could have lost his limbs, but he was lucky and he's very aware of that, so now he fundraises for research—well, the whole family do, he makes sure of it. The house and gardens are open to the public alternate weekends during the summer and they hold events in the park and split the proceeds between the charities and the estate.'

'Gosh, that sounds like a lot of hard work.'

'It is. Will's the estate manager, so he just incorporates it into his workload, and Mum oversees the garden and the house, but it's pretty much a full-time job for them keeping the place ticking over. And one day it'll be my job.'

She detected a note of resignation in his voice and tipped her head on one side enquiringly. 'You don't sound thrilled.'

He laughed. 'I'm not. I have a job, in case you haven't noticed, but I'm the oldest, so I get the short straw. Not for a while, though. Dad's only sixty-three and he's as fit as a flea, so between them hopefully they'll struggle on for a good few years yet.'

'I take it your brother will be there this weekend?'

'Will? Oh, yes. And his wife Sally. She's their events manager at the moment, but she'll be off for the summer on maternity leave, which should make life interesting.'

'I'm sure. Will they cope without her?'

He chuckled. 'I have no idea, but I'm not volunteering, I can assure you. I have quite enough to do.'

'I imagine you do. Does your brother know you're bringing me, by the way?'

He turned towards her, and in the dim light she could

see his eyebrow twitch. 'As in, did I tell him I'm bringing a girl? Yes. Did I mention why? No.'

She smiled at that. 'Won't he think it's odd?'

'That I have a social life? No. Should he?'

'No, of course not, but I didn't mean that.' She shrugged. 'I meant—I don't know—that none of them have ever heard of me. Won't there be a lot of speculation? Most people wouldn't turn up for their mother's sixtieth birthday with a total stranger in tow.'

'They would if they had my mother,' he said drily, making her laugh. 'And anyway, speculation is the general idea, isn't it?'

'Probably.' She rested her head back and looked across at him. 'Tell me about your mother, I'm sure she can't be that bad,' she said, and listened to him talking about his parents and his childhood with great affection. They were obviously a close-knit and loving family, and she envied them that. Her father was dead, her mother was remarried and lived in blissful penury in Ireland with her artist husband, and she and her married elder sister hardly ever spoke. It wasn't that they didn't like each other, but with seven years and several hundred miles between them, they had little in common, and the last time she'd seen her had been at a great-aunt's funeral a few months ago—a gathering that had opened a potentially devastating can of worms.

'So that's us. My father, my mother, me, my brother and his wife and a whole horde of cats and dogs and horses and cattle and deer—I take it you're all right with dogs, by the way? We have quite a few.'

She pulled herself back to the present and put the troubling thoughts aside. 'I'm fine with dogs. I'd have one if I wasn't at work all day.'

'Ditto. Not to mention half the night.'

'Mmm. So tell me about Jacob. I know you're happier with him now but did you get last night off?'

He laughed and scrubbed his hand around the back of his neck. 'Sort of. His left leg was swelling a bit yesterday—that was why they paged me. They thought he might be getting compartment syndrome, but nothing came of it, and I popped in before I went home last night and I went in again early this morning and it seems to have settled. He's OK—well, orthopaedic-wise, anyway, for the moment. The head injury's still a bit of a worry and he might need further surgery later on his legs and pelvis if he makes it, but at least that's looking increasingly likely, thank goodness.'

'So will you have to go back over the weekend?' she asked, wondering whether he would abandon her to the mercy of his mother and the dowagers, or take her back to Audley with him, but he was shaking his head.

'No, I hope not. This leg is the only critical issue I can see that might involve me, so I might take a quick run back tomorrow to check him, but the team are pretty good and he was looking stable when I left.'

He turned his head and she caught the flash of teeth as he smiled. 'Don't worry, I won't abandon you. I'll leave you with Will, if I have to dash off. He'll look after you.'

'I'll look forward to meeting him. He sounds interesting.'

'He is, but I hope you're tough. He's got a wicked sense of humour and he's a bit of a tease, and I don't suppose for a moment he'll be subtle. Stand by to be quizzed.'

'I'm sure I'll cope,' she said drily. 'I manage the boys on the ward.'

That made him laugh, and as they turned off the road and rattled over a cattle grid, he threw her a grin. 'Ready for this?'

'As I'll ever be,' she said, although she wasn't really

sure. Not now she knew a little more about them and the scale of the estate. It was sounding grander by the minute. 'What do I call your mother?' she asked as an afterthought.

'Jane—and my father's Tony.'

Or Lord Ashenden. Or should it be Sir Tony? Sir Anthony? She had no idea. Was he a lord? An earl? A baron? A marquis?

The titles were confusing, the whole aristocratic hierarchy a mystery to her, and she resolved to find out more about it. Not that it would be necessary to know, after this weekend, of course, because it would never affect her again. She reminded herself of that as they pulled up in what looked like the courtyard of an old stable block and he cut the engine. So far, so good, she thought, looking around in the gloom. It didn't look too outrageously grand—except of course this was the back. The front was probably altogether different.

By the time she'd fumbled with the catch on her seat belt, the door was open and he was helping her out. 'Watch where you walk, it can be a bit uneven on the cobbles and you don't want to fall off your stilts and wring your ankle.'

'What about our cases?'

'I'll get them later, unless you want anything from yours now?' he said, and when she shook her head, he ushered her towards a well-lit doorway with a firm, steadying hand on her back.

'We'll see if Will and Sally are still here—they've got the east wing,' he said, and she just about stopped her jaw dropping. The east wing? Good grief! Well, she'd known it was big, but for some reason it was only just starting to sink in *how* big, and she realised her whole house would probably fit into one of the stables!

'Shop!' he yelled, banging on the door, and it swung in

to reveal a younger version of him, slightly taller, identical ice-blue eyes mocking as he scanned his brother's face.

'You're cutting it a bit fine, aren't you?'

'Yeah, well, some of us have to go to work. And it's not as if you're in there already.'

'I have been. I came back to check the dog and ring you. Ma was starting to panic. Hi, you must be Libby,' he said, turning the full force of his charm on her. 'Come on in. I'm Will,' he said, and shook her hand firmly. He was looking intrigued and curious and welcoming all at once, and she smiled back, relishing the strength of his grip and utterly charmed by his smile and frank, assessing eyes—eyes just like his brother's.

'Hello, Will. It's good to meet you. Andrew's just been telling me a bit about you.'

'It'll all be lies,' he said with a grin. 'So—how come my brother's failed to mention you? Is he keeping you a deep, dark secret from Ma?'

She chuckled. 'I couldn't possibly comment,' she said lightly, and he laughed.

'You don't need to. Discreet isn't the word—getting information out of him is like getting blood out of a stone,' he said with a grin, and then stepped aside to let a great, shaggy grey dog through. 'This is Lara. Are you all right with dogs?'

'I'm fine with dogs. Hello, Lara. Aren't you gorgeous?'

'No, she's a pain,' Will said affectionately as the lurcher thrashed her long, skinny tail against his leg and slurped Libby's hand. 'She's a terrible thief, so I've cleverly trained her to steal my father's newspapers every morning, but the downside is if we leave anything on the worktop, she eats it.'

Libby laughed and rubbed the dog's head. 'Oh, darling, are you a naughty girl?' she murmured, and Lara slurped her again with her tongue.

'You'd better believe it,' Andrew said drily, then sighed. 'Come on, then, I suppose we ought to go and get this over with. Where's Sally?'

'In the kitchen trying to stop Ma interfering with the caterers. Come on, let's go and find them and then the birthday girl can make her grand entrance.'

Leaving the mournful Lara on the other side of a door, Will ushered them down a corridor into what was obviously the main part of the house, and then Andrew took her coat, putting it on a hook beside his as they went through into a huge and beautifully equipped kitchen and a scene of organised pandemonium.

'Andrew, darling! At last—I thought you were going to make some weak excuse about work like you usually do!'

'I don't know what you mean,' he teased. He bent his head and kissed his mother's cheek, hugging her gently, and then turned and drew Libby forward.

'Mum, this is Libby Tate. Libby, my mother, Jane.'

Lady Ashenden was elegant, beautifully groomed and she looked a little flustered. Her dark hair was threaded with silver, swept up into a smooth pleat—unlike Libby's own which was twisted up and skewered more or less in place with faux-ivory pins—and she realised that Andrew and Will both had her eyes.

Piercing eyes, searching, which turned on her and seemed, to Libby's relief, to like what they saw, because she embraced her warmly and kissed her cheeks. 'Libby, welcome to Ashenden. This is Sally, my daughter-in-law.'

Sally was small, obviously pregnant and had the same friendly openness as Will. She buzzed Libby's cheek and grinned. 'Hi, there. Welcome to the madhouse. I'll look forward to catching up with you later, but in the meantime, Jane, isn't it time we went up?'

'I'm sure it is. They don't need us in here fussing and you've done enough, darling. Let's leave them to it, I'm sure they can cope without us.'

And Jane turned away from her, missing the eye-rolling and laughter that passed between her and Will, and the intimate smile which followed as Will drew the pregnant woman up against his side and hugged her tenderly. They were obviously very much in love, Libby thought, and felt a wash of restless longing. If only there was someone in her life who felt like that about her, but even if there was, there would be no guarantee they'd have Will and Sally's happy ending.

The question-mark hanging over her future loomed again, but there wasn't time to dwell on it, and as they left the kitchen and walked along a magnificent curved hallway with tall, elegant windows overlooking the floodlit front of the house, she was brought firmly back to the here and now as the scale of the house began to register.

Amy hadn't been exaggerating, Libby thought. It really was a stately home—a vast, magnificent, Palladian country house, the centre part built in a crescent around a carriage-sweep at the front of the house, and as they reached the entrance hall, bracketed by broad, sweeping stairs that led up towards an ornate domed ceiling soaring far above them, Jane led them across a rug that would no doubt have been priceless if it hadn't been worn thin by the passage of generations, and through an open doorway.

As soon as they entered the drawing room—jaw-dropping in its proportions and dripping with antiques and old masters—they were swept into a round of introductions and fleeting, meaningless conversations. They lost Sally and Will somewhere along the way, and then Andrew grabbed two glasses of champagne from a passing waiter, steered her into a quiet corner and gave her a rueful smile.

'Sorry, it's a bit full on if you're not used to it.'

Full on? She was utterly out of her depth! 'I thought it was just dinner?' she murmured, and he laughed.

'It is dinner, but there's nothing just about it. Dinner will be about forty people, and tomorrow will be a couple of hundred, I expect. Possibly more. And she'll know every last one of them and the names of all their children and dogs and horses—she's a legend.'

'And she wants to see you married.'

'Mmm. All ready to take over this crumbling old heap of dry rot.'

'Are you whingeing about the ancestral home again, bro'?' Will murmured from behind them, and he gave a soft snort and turned to him.

'Would I? Thankfully they're both looking well, so I don't have to worry about it for donkey's years. Have you got a drink?'

'No, but I'll have champagne, if you're offering, and I expect Sally'll have some elderflower cordial. Don't worry about Libby, I'll entertain her while you're gone.'

Libby met Will's twinkling eyes as Andrew walked away to get the drinks. 'So, tell me about this crumbling old heap of dry rot. Does he really hate it?' she said to him, and he chuckled.

'Oh, he loves it to bits, really, but he thinks it should be mine, since I run it. The law of primogeniture offends his sense of right and wrong.'

'And yours?'

He shrugged casually. 'It's just one of those things, isn't it? If you split the estate with every generation, you end up with nothing left—and if you ask him about it, he'll tell you we're just caretakers, which is right. Glorified janitors. But he's welcome to the title—and frankly he's welcome to the house. The east wing is much nicer—I still get to enjoy the grounds, but it's cosier than the house, and the heating bills aren't quite as stratospheric, and I can walk to work. And whatever he's told you, I only run the estate because I'm too lazy to do anything else!'

They were laughing as Andrew returned, a ripple of interest following him as the single girls monitored his progress. Or was it Will they were interested in? She couldn't blame them. Both men were strikingly good-looking and she felt completely overshadowed in the glittering crowd of slender, elegant women with their bright, witty banter and designer dresses.

Until Sally came over a moment later, short and round and utterly charming, and smiled at her and gave her a hug.

'Finally I get to meet you properly! This is such fun, I didn't know my brother-in-law had a deep, dark secret.'

Andrew rolled his eyes. 'Just because I don't gossip.'

'Yeah, yeah,' Sally said, and took her by the arm mischievously. 'So—tell all. I gather you're colleagues. That must be tricky. What's he like to work with, because his brother's a nightmare—'

'I am not!'

'You are. You're hopelessly disorganised.'

Will grinned. 'That's why I employed you.'

'No, it's why you married me. You were terrified I'd leg it and you wouldn't find anyone else who could cope with your filing system.'

'It's a good system!'

'It's a collection of piles on the floor, William!' she corrected with a grin, and Libby laughed.

'Sounds rather like my desk,' she said with a smile at

Will, then turned back to Sally. 'So what do you actually do? Andrew said something about being events manager.'

'Oh, that's just a fancy title for doing anything and everything. I'm just a dogsbody,' she grumbled cheerfully, but Will shook his head.

'She's actually my PA as well, and she helps me run the charity side of things, too,' Will said. 'We'd be lost without her—will be lost when she has the baby, but it's not why I married her. I married her because I struggle to boil water and she's a darned good cook.'

And rather more than that, Libby wouldn't mind guessing, hearing the pride in his voice and seeing the warmth in his eyes as he smiled at Sally, and yet again, she felt a twinge of envy.

If only Andrew would look at her like that—would ever, in the future, look at her like that—but he wouldn't. Why would he? Their worlds were light-years apart. He'd only invited her here this weekend as an afterthought. He'd never noticed her before, never singled her out, never been anything but the perfect colleague. She was only here because he needed a shield, and he'd made that perfectly clear.

Not that she needed to worry. She wasn't in the market for a relationship either at the moment, with him or with anybody else, and she'd do well to remember that fact.

# CHAPTER THREE

HER thoughts were interrupted as they all filed through to the dining room, and she found herself seated at a long table between a jovial, middle-aged man who looked like a farmer, and Will.

Andrew was opposite her, and as she looked up and caught his eye he sent her a slow wink and she felt his foot slide against hers.

Playing footsie? Playing 'let's pretend'? Or giving her moral support?

The latter, she realised as he withdrew his foot and started talking to Sally, and she suppressed a little pang of disappointment as she turned to the man on her right with a smile. 'Hello, I'm Libby Tate,' she said.

'Ah, yes, Andrew's girl. You're breaking hearts all round this table, I hope you realise?' he said softly, and held out his hand. 'Chris Turner. We're neighbours and old friends of the family. It's nice to meet you, Libby—very nice. I always knew he'd settle down in his own time, and it's good to see him looking happy.'

Oh, good grief. What on earth was she supposed to say to that? Nothing, apparently. Chris just winked and sat back with a kindly smile. 'So, tell me, what do you do?'

'I'm a ward sister on Paediatrics. I work alongside Andrew at the Audley Memorial Hospital.'

'Ah. A *real* person. That explains it all.'

She frowned in confusion, and Chris chuckled.

'My wife Louise and I have watched the boys grow up, and we always knew they'd go their own way. Why Andrew's taken so long I can't imagine, but I expect he was just waiting for the right woman.'

'Are you stirring, Turner?' Andrew said from across the table where he'd clearly been watching and lip-reading, and Chris chuckled again.

'Of course not. Would I?'

'Probably. It's all lies, Libby. You don't want to listen to anything he says.'

She did, though, because he was telling her all sorts of fascinating things about Andrew, and she was hanging on his every word. It emerged that far from being a farmer, Chris was a GP, the Ashendens' family doctor, his wife the local vicar, and he told her hilarious stories of Andrew's childhood, the humour fading at one point as he talked about Will's illness, and how much it had affected Andrew, who'd been at medical school at the time.

'He changed then. He used to be a bit of a wild child, but then suddenly, it was as if the joy went out of him.'

'Because of Will?' she asked, her voice hushed.

Chris shrugged. 'Who knows? But he's a good man,' he said softly. 'If Will hadn't recovered so well I'm sure he would have chucked in his career to come home and help care for him if it had been necessary. It's the sort of thing he'd do without a second thought, but he never talks about it. He just gets on with it, no matter what it costs him in terms of time and effort, and when Will recovered so well, he threw himself back into medicine and he's been focussed on it ever since, to the exclusion of everything else. He's a fantastically dedicated doctor—but you already know that. I'm preaching to the converted.'

'Oh, you are. He's amazing,' she agreed thoughtfully. She'd seen him at work, seen how dedicated he was, and it made sense now—the close way he followed up his young patients, the passionate zeal with which he directed their treatment, the dedicated focus on his career. No wonder he didn't have a wife and family. He simply didn't have time.

But Chris was right, she'd seen him smile more in the last day or two than she had in all the previous months she'd known him. Was that down to her? No, surely not. He was just showing her another side of himself, a side that Chris had maybe not seen recently.

She glanced up at Andrew and caught his eye, and he winked at her, then turned back to Will. That he had a very close bond with his younger brother was blindingly obvious from the banter that was taking place between them now across the table. The teasing affection between them brought a lump to her throat and she wanted to talk to Will, to hear more from him about Andrew, and when Chris's attention was taken by the lady on his other side, Will turned towards her and gave her a rueful grin.

'Sorry, I've been neglecting you,' he said.

'Don't worry,' she said, smiling back. 'Chris has been looking after me. You can pay me back in a minute, though, I'm struggling to work out which knife and fork I need next,' she added in an undertone, and he laughed out loud, making Andrew frown curiously at them.

'Frightful, isn't it?' he said with a playful wince. 'Starting at the outside and working inwards is usually a good plan, but if you want to be sure, watch Andrew, not me. He's pretty good on the old protocol, but I don't care.

Frankly I don't have a lot of time for it. I'm much more interested in the people.' His eyes flicked over her, the curiosity in them undisguised. 'On the subject of which, how long have you known my brother?' he murmured, and she felt her heart lurch a little.

Here we go, she thought, determined not to lie and hoping he wouldn't put her in the position where she had to. 'Six months,' she told him, 'since he started at the hospital.'

'Good grief, the dark horse,' he said slowly, shooting a glance in Andrew's direction. 'Still, I can see why he'd want to keep you to himself, but it's too late now, he's rumbled. You can save me a dance tomorrow night. Rumour has it I'm better than him.'

'I wonder who started that rumour?' she teased, but then confessed, 'I wouldn't know what he's like. We haven't danced together yet.' Or anything else apart from work, come to that, she thought with another hitch in her pulse, but Will didn't need to know that.

'Well, here's your chance. You can dance with us both and judge for yourself. Not that you'd be disloyal and unkind enough to tell either of us the truth,' he said with gentle mockery. 'So—tell me about yourself, Libby Tate. What makes you tick?'

'Oh, there's nothing to tell,' she said lightly, wondering what Andrew would have told him and how much of it she was going to contradict if she said anything, but Will just smiled.

'I'll just bet there is,' he said, his voice still low. 'I think you're probably a complex and fascinating woman, but I get the feeling he doesn't know much about you, either. Curious.'

Suddenly she couldn't do this—couldn't lie to his brother, pretend they were together when they weren't. Not like that, anyway—and not when he'd already worked it out.

'We haven't been going out together long,' she admitted, for Andrew's sake not revealing just how brief their non-relationship was, but Will just nodded and smiled slightly.

'No. I thought not. Correct me if I'm wrong, but I've got a sneaking suspicion you're only here as a smoke-screen to disguise the fact that he doesn't have a social life—or am I mistaken?'

She felt her cheeks heat, and he chuckled softly. 'Don't worry, your secret's safe with me, and maybe that is why he's invited you, but I get the feeling there's more to it—or at least, maybe you'd like there to be, and I can see Andrew would.'

She opened her mouth to protest, but he just arched a brow slightly and murmured, 'Just so you know, I probably ought to warn you Ma's put you together in his room.'

Her fork slipped through her fingers, and he caught it between his hand and the edge of the table, meeting her shocked eyes with a grin. 'Steady, now,' he murmured, then his smile softened. 'Don't worry, there's a hideously uncomfortable divan in the dressing room. He'll sleep on that, he's nothing if not a gentleman.'

Did she want that? She met Andrew's watchful eyes across the table, and suddenly she wasn't so sure. She wondered if he'd known about their sleeping arrangements before, and decided probably not. He was too straightforward to be devious, that much she did know about him, and he'd promised her no strings.

So would he take the divan? Or break his promise?

Divan, she realised, and felt a flicker of something that could easily have been disappointment.

Andrew thought the dinner would never end.

Libby was sandwiched between his brother and Chris

Turner, and one after the other they were telling tales about him. He knew this from the mocking glances he kept getting from Will, and the active curiosity of Chris's steady, unruffled gaze.

He had no idea what Will was asking her. She'd blushed at one point and shot him a slightly desperate glance, but there was nothing he could do about it in the way of damage limitation from the other side of the table. He'd just have to talk to her later and find out what he'd said. Of course, if he'd been sitting next to her…

At last, when his nerves were stretched to breaking point, the meal came to and end and they all headed for the drawing room, and as soon as he could he reached Libby's side and slid a possessive arm around her waist, giving her a reassuring squeeze.

'Hi. Have you survived?' he murmured.

She laughed brightly, but a soft blush touched her cheeks and sent his blood pressure rocketing. 'Of course. Your brother and Chris have been fascinating dinner companions.'

'I'm sure,' he said drily. 'I should have got to the seating plan.'

'No, that was me,' Will said with a grin that made Libby feel distinctly nervous. 'I wanted to get to know your new woman.'

'Did you. Well, what a surprise. More coffee, Libby, or another drink?'

She shook her head. 'No, I don't need any more alcohol and the coffee'll keep me awake and I'm wilting on my feet, I'm afraid. Would it be dreadfully rude to turn in?'

'Not at all, I think it sounds an excellent idea. I'll get our cases in from the car and we can make ourselves scarce. Will, do you have any idea where Mum's put us?'

'Your room.'

Just that. Nothing more, except for the knowing look in Will's eyes, and Andrew stifled a groan, nodded curtly and turned to Libby. 'I'll get the luggage and come back for you,' he said, and left her there with Will and Sally while he headed for the back stairs and the way out to the car.

Damn. He couldn't believe his mother would have done that, but maybe she'd thought she was being broad-minded. After all, he was thirty-four. It wouldn't be unlikely that he'd be sharing a room with his girlfriend.

Only she wasn't his girlfriend, more's the pity, and he had rather expected his mother to be more old-fashioned about it.

Damn, damn, damn!

He hauled their cases out of the boot of his car, plipped the remote and took them up to his room.

Flowers. Flowers on the chest of drawers. He'd *never* had flowers in his room—but come to that, he'd never stayed here with a woman. He realised in shock that it was the first time he'd ever brought a woman home—well, if you didn't count innocent teenage flings and friends from college, which he didn't—and he'd had no idea how his mother would react.

Or overreact.

He stuck his head round the corner into the dressing room and saw the small divan neatly made up, and he heaved a sigh of relief. She'd left his options open, bless her heart, and he was sure they'd cope. Except, of course, that the little bed was a heap of springs and far too small for his adult frame, but there was no way he'd ask Libby to sleep on it. It was out of the Spanish Inquisition.

He'd manage. There probably wasn't another option, anyway. The house would be bursting at the seams, even Will and Sally's spare rooms would have been pressed into service, and at least in this room they had the choice of sleeping arrangements. Not that it was much of a choice. He put his case on the hateful little daybed, hers on the big, comfortable half-tester in the main room, switched on the bedside lights and went back down to retrieve her, because he was running out of steam. Two sleepless nights on the trot were getting to him, and he had no idea if he'd be called back to the hospital tonight for little Jacob.

He hoped not. He'd only had one glass of champagne all evening just in case, and he'd left half of that, but if he didn't get his head down soon he'd be no good in an emergency anyway.

She was standing where he'd left her, engaged in conversation with his cousin Charlotte, and his heart sank. Charlotte was a nightmare. She'd had a crush on him for years, and she wouldn't be wasting any time laying her claim.

'Hi, Charlie,' he said, just to annoy her, and buzzed her cheek briefly before turning to Libby and sliding his arm around her waist and easing her closer. 'I'm sorry, you're going to have to excuse us, we're both bushed and we need an early night, don't we, darling?'

She tilted her face up to his and smiled, and only he could see the mockery in her eyes. 'Oh, yes, absolutely. Sorry. It's been lovely to meet you, Charlotte. Night, Will, night, Sally. See you tomorrow.'

And slipping her arm around his waist, she wriggled closer and let him steer her towards the stairs.

'Darling?' she murmured under her breath, shooting him a sideways look as they went together up the first step, and he chuckled.

'Sorry. That was for Cousin Charlotte's benefit.'

'Ahh. Would that be zillionth cousin Charlotte umpteen times removed, by any chance?' she said lightly, and he laughed again.

'That would be the one. I thought Will would have the sense to lose her for you.'

'I think Will imagined I could take care of myself,' she replied, easing out of his hold as soon as they'd turned the corner and were out of view. 'He also tells me you're a gentleman.'

He turned the knob and pushed the bedroom door open. 'Sadly, he's right,' he said, closing the door behind them and stifling a sigh of regret. 'I'll be sleeping round the corner. The bathroom's through there; I'll let you go first.'

She woke on Saturday morning to the sound of water running, and lay and listened as Andrew showered in the en suite bathroom which had been stolen from part of the adjoining dressing room where he'd spent the night, as she'd realised he would. It was still early—only half past seven, and they'd been up until after midnight, so she wondered if he'd had a call to go to the hospital.

No. He wouldn't be showering if that was the case, he'd just dress and run. A sunbeam slanted through a chink in the curtains, and she crept out of bed and opened them. It was a beautiful day—gloriously sunny, the sky a brilliant blue with scudding white clouds and the promise of spring.

But only the promise. She shivered a little, realising that the sunshine was deceptive. The heating was on—she could hear the pipes creaking, but the old house must be as leaky as a sieve and trying to heat it was inevitably to fight a losing battle. She could feel the draught around the window frame as she stood looking out across the rolling parkland towards the river in the distance. The willows by the river were bursting into leaf, and she could hear birds singing.

Beautiful, she thought, and smiled. Much better than

Paris, and she'd still get her riverside walk. Pity about her cream jumper…

The bathroom door opened and Andrew walked out, naked except for a towel wrapped round his waist and looking bright-eyed and bushy-tailed and full of the joys of spring. And mouthwateringly gorgeous.

He grinned at her. 'Morning. I didn't expect that you'd be up yet. I hope I didn't wake you.'

She shook her head. 'Not really. I never sleep late, and to be honest it's so quiet here it's a little eerie. There isn't a soul about, only the birds.'

'Will's sure to be up. He always rides first thing, and he's bound to be out today—it's a gorgeous day.'

She dragged her eyes off his chest. 'So I see,' she replied, turning back to the window and trying not to think too much about that broad, muscular expanse under the scatter of dark hair glistening with water droplets. 'Can we go for that walk you were talking about?'

'Sure. I'll throw my clothes on and leave you to get ready. I'll be in the kitchen. I take it you can find your way?'

'I'm sure I'll manage. I'll ring you on your mobile if I get lost,' she joked. 'Down the stairs and along the corridor?'

'Go the easy way—turn left, straight to the end of the landing, down the back stairs and the kitchen's at the bottom,' he told her. 'I'll go and get the kettle on—do you want breakfast now or do you want to wait for the whole full English shindig with kippers and scrambled egg and Cousin Charlotte?'

She laughed and turned away from the window. 'I think we can avoid Cousin Charlotte. You do realise she's in love with you, do you?'

He gave a wry smile. 'Oh, yes. She tells me every time she gets me alone, which is as infrequently as I can manage it. She's been in love with me for years. So—fancy a cooked breakfast? I can probably rustle something up.'

Libby shook her head. 'No, I'm still full from last night. I'll have a quick shower and join you in a minute, then could we have tea and toast?'

'Sure. I'll give you ten minutes.' He went into the dressing room, pulling on a pair of well-worn jeans and his weary old loafers to the sound of running water in the shower, dragging a jumper over his head as he headed for the door and tried not to think of what she was doing behind the bathroom door.

He needed to get out of there, to suck some air into his lungs and forget about how she'd looked when he'd woken, her hair trailed across her pillow, the soft, silky strands fanned out against the white Egyptian cotton, her lashes lying like crescents against her pale cheeks—and then just a few minutes later, standing in front of the window with the early morning sun behind her, outlining her body perfectly through the fine fabric of her night-dress. Her long and perfectly respectable nightdress—if you didn't count the effect of the sunlight streaming through it...

He went down to the kitchen and let the dogs out, then put the kettle on the Aga and hummed softly as it boiled. There was a mountain of bread of every description in the larder, and he chose a lovely nutty wholemeal, sliced it and sandwiched it in the wire toasting gadget and clamped it under the hob cover, flipping it after a minute to toast the other side, and as he pulled it out the door opened and Libby came in, looking fresh as a daisy and squeaky-clean, and he just wanted to hug her.

Instead, he smiled, poured boiling water on the tea bags and stacked the toast on a plate in the middle of the battered old table. 'Just shove the dogs out of the way and sit down. Jam, marmalade, honey or Marmite?'

'Oh, marmalade, please. Thanks. That smells fantastic. Hello, dogs, aren't you lovely? Oh, tea—bless you!'

And she buried her nose in the mug and breathed deeply, her fingers wrapped round it, the steam drifting around her like a wraith, and he wanted her as he hadn't wanted a woman in years.

Or maybe for ever…

It really was the most gorgeous day. The wind was chilly, but she was well wrapped up. Andrew had kitted her out in borrowed wellies and a thick, warm jacket, and he took her down to the river, as he'd promised.

'This is lovely,' she sighed, leaning against a fence and staring out over the lightly ruffled water. The sunlight was sparkling on it, and she could see birds bobbing about near the shore.

He propped his elbows on the rail beside her and gave her a wry smile. 'I'm sorry it's not the Seine.'

'Oh, no, don't be sorry, it's beautiful,' she murmured, watching a swan circling lazily in the water. 'So peaceful—it's bliss. I can't think of anything better.'

He smiled, and they strolled on, the dogs milling around and sniffing, and Lara appeared out of nowhere and joined them, the three of them racing off into the undergrowth after a rabbit.

'Will can't be far away,' Andrew said, and a few moments later they heard the drum of approaching hoof-beats. Will pulled up alongside them, grinning down at them as the bay mare caught her breath, sides heaving, chest wet and flecked with foam.

'Morning!'

Libby smiled up at him. 'Good morning. What a lovely day.'

'Been somewhere in a hurry?' Andrew asked mildly, eyeing the sweaty horse, but Will just laughed.

'We went round the new cross-country course again. She's brilliant, I love her.'

'I thought she was a temperamental cow?'

He laughed again. 'She was—last week. That's women for you, but she's the bravest horse I've ever had. You ought to take her for a ride, you'll love her.'

'I'll take your word for it, she's a bit feisty for me,' Andrew said, patting the mare's wet, steaming neck and rubbing her nose. 'I'm getting too old to break things, and so are you.'

'Rubbish, you're just a coward and, anyway, she's a schoolmistress, safe as houses. I'd put a child on her.'

'I shouldn't tell Sally that,' he muttered drily, but Will just laughed.

'Seen Lara, by the way? She's messed off again.'

'Oh, she's around somewhere. She got distracted by a rabbit and went off with the others. We'll bring her back.'

'No, she'll come, she won't want to miss breakfast. We're having bacon and she's already clocked it, the thief. Sally only just got there first. Never trust a lurcher, Libby,' he advised with a grin, then he turned in the saddle and let out a piercing whistle, and Lara came bounding up, tongue lolling, grinning cheerfully. She'd obviously had a lovely run, and with a wave Will turned his mare towards the house and made his way back at a much more sedate pace, Lara trotting at the horse's heels.

'Is your brother a bit of a daredevil?' Libby asked thoughtfully, watching him ride away, and Andrew gave a grunt of laughter.

'Just a bit. Fortunately, he's got the most natural seat I've ever seen, and he just stays stuck—which is a good job, because he's got more courage than sense and he gives Mum and Sally fits. I thought with the baby coming, maybe he'd settle down, become a bit more responsible, but he's just crazy. That's how he got into the charity thing—he was doing sky-dives and bungee-jumps and marathons, stuff like that, and it occurred to him he could raise money doing it, so it sort of legitimises his lunacy.'

'So what does Sally think of it?'

He shrugged. 'She just grits her teeth, but I know she's getting more worried. I mean, it's not just her now, is it, and sometimes I think he hasn't got a shred of responsibility.'

'Is it just a reaction to his illness?' she asked, thinking about what Chris had said the night before, and Andrew nodded.

'Yes. Well, I think so, in a way. He didn't die, he got away with it, so he thinks he can get away with anything. Only one day he'll find out he can't, and then Sally will be left picking up the pieces.'

They strolled on for a while, but the wind off the water was chilly, even with a thick jacket on, so they turned away from the river, heading back across the park to the house by a different route. And as they walked, she got her first real appreciation of the scale of the house and its grounds—his heritage, his destiny and, extraordinarily, his home. It was just another world and, beautiful though it was, she didn't envy him any of it for an instant. Except maybe the peace and quiet and the sense of space. That was really special.

They went through a little wood, and startled a small herd of deer. They lifted their heads, stood motionless for a second and then bounded away, leaving her entranced. 'Oh—how lovely,' she murmured. 'They're beautiful!'

'Yes, they are. They're a bit destructive, though. Mum constantly wages war on them. They get into the garden and cause havoc. So do the rabbits, which we're overrun with. One of the drawbacks of the sandy soil, I'm afraid, but the garden's walled, so it's not as bad as it could be.'

They emerged from the wood and he stopped her with his hand on her arm. 'Look—can you see the folly?'

She looked where he was pointing, but she couldn't see anything. Not until he came right up beside her. 'There—look along my arm,' he murmured, leaning closer so she could do that, the warmth of his body surrounding her. She breathed deeply, drawing in the scent of his skin, and then she opened her eyes and there it was, a little circular building sheltering on the edge of another small wood some distance away.

'Oh, it's pretty!'

'It is—it's delightful. Completely useless, but delightful. My great-grandfather's idea, apparently. He built it for his wife, but she hated it. Called it lewd and uncivilised and refused to go there.'

'Strange woman. I think it's lovely.'

'So do I, but she had a point. I'll show you later, if we've got time.'

They joined a track cutting across the park, and as they approached the house, she saw it from the front for the first time, with the huge green copper dome that must be above that beautiful ceiling in the entrance hall, and it took her breath away. It was glorious. Magnificent—and a terrifying responsibility. No wonder he was daunted by it—or at least, if not daunted, fighting against the inevitability of it.

She could see people milling about, vans being un-loaded, others arriving, and here and there a group of people strolling on the grass. She recognised some of them from the night before, and realised they were the guests. The others were much more businesslike, engaged, she imagined, on preparing the house for the ball.

'So what happens for the rest of the day?' she asked, wondering how she'd cope if they had to go shooting, for example, but his words reassured her.

'Oh, I'm sure there'll be a packed programme of activities for anyone who can be bothered. We can join in, if you want, or keep our heads down and chill. Up to you.'

'Chill?' she suggested tentatively, horribly aware of how grand it all was and how out of her depth she'd felt last night amongst all the socialite butterflies, and he flashed her a smile.

'That would be my preference,' he said honestly, 'but I don't want you to be bored.'

'Oh, I won't be bored,' she assured him instantly. 'How could I be bored? Look at it! It's so beautiful here, all this stunning countryside.'

His mouth lifted in a wry smile. 'All I see is a pile of responsibilities stretching away into the hereafter. It should go to Will, really. He's the one who loves it, the one with the vision. He knows every inch of it far better than I ever will. You ought to ask him to give you a guided tour.'

'I'd rather you showed me.'

His smile softened. 'So would I. We'll take a drive this afternoon, go for a walk in the woods—we could have lunch out, if you like, rather than stay here. There's a pub in the village down on the river, it's rather nice. Or we can take a picnic and eat it in the folly. I'm sure there's something in one of the fridges we can steal.'

'Shouldn't we be here for lunch? The dutiful son and all that?' she asked, but he shook his head, his eyes glinting with mischief.

'Only if you want to brave Charlie again.'

'Oh, poor Charlotte. I think I'll pass,' she said with a contrite smile. 'I feel so guilty when she tells me you're virtually engaged.'

'Don't. It's just her wishful thinking, she'll get over it one day.'

'In which case, a picnic in the folly sounds perfect. Won't the caterers mind if you raid the fridge, though?'

His smile widened. 'No,' he said confidently. 'We'll steal it from the family kitchen. The caterers for tonight's extravaganza will be working in the visitors' centre— they've got a big catering kitchen over there and it's perfect for such a large function, but the cooks who work in the visitors' centre restaurant will be doing lunch in the house, and they won't mind if we steal something from the buffet stash. They love me.'

His grin was cocky and boyish and endearing, and she could easily see how they might indeed love him. It wouldn't be hard at all, she thought wistfully, and felt sorry for Charlotte all over again.

They went in through the back door, into the family kitchen where they'd had breakfast with the dogs, and found breakfast cleared away and the team of cooks in full swing preparing lunch for the house guests; they greeted him with smiles and told him to help himself, so Andrew swiped a few slices of asparagus and mushroom quiche still warm from the oven, a bowl of salad and a handful of crusty rolls, put them in a basket with a bottle of spring water and some plastic cups and a bunch of grapes and some cheese, and they headed off in the car. She took her borrowed boots and jacket, and they drove to the edge of a wood, parked the car and walked to the folly.

'Oh, it's beautiful! The walls are all painted!' she ex-

claimed, her eyes wide as she stepped inside and stared
around.

He saw the moment she registered the content, the soft
colour that swept her cheeks, the muffled laugh through
fingers pressed lightly against her lips. 'I understand now
why she thought it was lewd and uncivilised, but really
they're lovely,' she said, turning to him with a smile, and
he smiled back, watching her as she looked again at the
paintings of naked lovers frolicking in the woods; her eyes
were entranced, and he was pleased he'd brought her
here—pleased he'd had the idea of the picnic and that she
hadn't wanted to do all the tedious and organised things
that the others would be doing. This way he had her to
himself, but the downside was they were alone in a room
designed for lovers, a room filled with images that heated
his imagination and made his thoughts run riot.

Thoughts filled with images of him and Libby.

And that was worrying. It wasn't supposed to be like
this; she was there for show, not for him to sneak away with
alone and have more fun than he'd had in years, frolicking
in the folly surrounded by nymphs in gauzy gowns flitting
through the fading scenery. The memory of her this morning with the sun streaming through her fine cotton nightdress hit him in the solar plexus, and his breath jammed in
his throat.

'It'll be warmer outside,' he said, suddenly desperate to
get away from the paintings, so they went back out into the
sunshine and sat down on the steps, looking out over a bend
in the river in the distance, and they ate the picnic slowly,
savouring the view, somehow not needing to talk. So refresh-
ing, he thought, to sit with her and not to fill the silence.

A squirrel came up to them, head tilted slightly on one
side, and she threw it a tiny crumb of quiche.

'Feeding the wildlife?' he murmured, and the squirrel grabbed it and fled, darting up a tree and disappearing.

'It's probably got young,' she said.

'Probably. Are you all done?'

'Mmm. That was lovely, thank you. Much nicer than being polite to poor little Charlotte. So what now?'

'I can show you the bits we didn't get to this morning, if you like?'

'Sounds good.'

'Let's go, then,' he said, packing up the things and getting to his feet. They walked and drove and walked again, and despite everything he'd said about the place, she could see that he loved it.

It was in his blood, in his bones. How could he not love it? And yet he was right, it was an awesome responsibility, and as he talked about it, about how they were merely caretakers for the future generations, about the struggle to make ends meet, the difficulties of opening the house and gardens to the public, the rules and regulations, the health and safety implications, she could see how it could be a love-hate relationship.

'It must be a nightmare opening to the public,' she mused as they stood and looked at the house across the wide expanse of the park. 'I can't imagine anything more stressful than having people wandering through my home touching everything. Do you use all the rooms and have to clear them up the night before?'

He laughed softly and shook his head. 'No. The ones we open are the big rooms that we don't use that much, and now Will's in the east wing and I don't live here any more it's much easier. Visitors don't have access to all the house, by any means, and the walkways are all roped off to corral them a bit, but there's always the odd one who tries to escape from the guides. There's a bedroom Queen Victoria stayed in and the old nursery, and the drawing room and dining room we used last night, and of course the ballroom, which you'll see later. That's gorgeous. And the old Victorian kitchen. That's next to the family kitchen and it's lovely, but it's never used. It's just a museum piece now, like one of the bathrooms and some of the other bits like part of the stable block and the old coach house, but it's all pretty strung out so they feel they've seen more than they have, really.'

Another kitchen? That made three—four if she counted Will and Sally's. 'Don't you ever get lost?' she asked, slightly dazed, but he just smiled and shook his head.

'No. I grew up here, don't forget, and Will and I had the run of the place.'

'I bet you were a nightmare.'

'Who, me? No way,' he said, eyes alight with mischief, and she could just imagine him as an eight-year-old, all skinned knees and sparkling eyes and wicked little grin, ricocheting from one scrape to another.

And just the thought was enough to make her heart ache. If she was lucky, then one day she might have a son, a little boy like Andrew must have been—but that all depended on which way the dice had fallen, and until she knew…

She shivered as the wind picked up and the temperature dropped, and he realised he'd rambled on and kept her out in the wind for ages. 'I'm sorry, you're cold—have you seen enough?' he asked, and she nodded, so they headed back towards the car. She snuggled down inside the jacket and turned the collar up, and he looked at the glow in her cheeks and the sparkle in her eyes, and felt a surge of regret that this wasn't a real relationship, that they were in his room together under false pretences and that once they returned to Audley tomorrow it would all come to an end and they'd go back to normal, him the overworked, harassed consultant, her the overworked but always cheerful ward sister.

Hell, it was going to be hard to do that. He'd forgotten what they were supposed to be doing, had let himself get carried away by the moment and spent the day having fun with her—good, clean, healthy fun, free of ties and responsibilities and obligations, and it had been wonderful.

He wanted to pull her into his arms and kiss her, to fold her against his chest and hold her tight, just stand there with her in his arms while time stood still and the world moved on without them. But he couldn't. He had responsibilities that day, and he'd shirked them long enough. The ball was taken care of, but he had a duty to the other guests, and his mother was probably going to hang him out to dry if he didn't get back there soon.

Either that or she'd be planning the wedding.

He unlocked the car, opened the door for her and as she slid in and reached for the seat belt their eyes met and she smiled.

'Thank you, Andrew. I've had the best day,' she said, and he just couldn't help himself. He leant in and kissed her—the lightest, slightest brush of his lips against hers, but his heart kicked hard against his ribs and blood surged through him.

He stepped back and shut the door a little more firmly than was necessary, went round and slid behind the wheel and drove home in silence, regret for what could never be wedged like a ball in his throat.

If the dinner party had been a glittering occasion, the ball that night promised to be a firework display. The place had been a hive of activity from dawn onwards, and the pace had only picked up as the day went on. Now, though, was the lull before the storm. The cars and vans were gone or parked out of sight, the stage was set, and she felt a tingle of excitement. She'd never been to a white-tie ball before, and she was assailed by doubts about Amy's dress.

Oh, well, nothing she could do about it now. It was all she had with her and it would have to do.

Andrew changed first. He disappeared into his dressing room and emerged in trousers and a shirt hanging open down the front. The wing collar was attached, but the stiffly starched front was meant to close with studs. The studs he had in his hand.

'Can you put these in for me? This shirt is an instrument of torture and I just can't do it. There's a pocket here you can put your hand in to make it easier to reach,' he demonstrated, and so she found herself nose to nose with his warm, solid, muscular chest, breathing in the scent of cologne and soap and, underlying it all, the drugging, masculine scent of his body.

Following his instructions, she put the first stud through from the back and her fingers brushed against the soft scatter of dark hair, sending heat coursing through her.

Darn it, how could he do this to her? She was almost whimpering by the time she'd fastened the last one, her fingers against the shirt front picking up the steady, even beat of his heart, the warmth of his body, the solidity, while the subtle spicy tones of his aftershave curled around her nostrils and teased her.

Andrew was struggling, too, the feel of her fingers tormenting him unbearably. 'All done,' she said at last, and he thanked her, stepping back the moment her hands fell away, and wheeled round and disappeared to assemble the rest of his elaborate and formal dress.

He wondered if she had any idea of the effect she had on him. Watching her, her soft, full bottom lip caught between her even white teeth, feeling her slender fingers brush against his chest, inhaling the scent of apples that drifted from her hair—it had been enough to kill him. And he was going to have to dance with her tonight. It would be expected, by her, by his mother, and most particularly by all the women who'd like to be in her place.

Maybe she'd hate dancing and they could sit it out, he thought, clutching at straws, but he had a feeling Libby didn't hate anything. She wasn't a wild party girl by any means, but she'd enjoyed herself last night, mixed easily with his friends and family, and he just knew she'd want to dance. Not that he didn't want to. Rather the opposite, but he just didn't trust himself to hold her in his arms without disgracing himself.

By the time he emerged in the long black tailcoat and white waistcoat over the satin-stripe trousers, his white bow-tie finally tied to his satisfaction, he'd managed to get himself back under control to a certain extent. 'Right, are you OK to get ready on your own or will you need help with anything?' he asked, hoping she'd say she could cope, and to his relief she nodded.

'I'll be fine.'

'Right. I'm going to help Will. He doesn't stand a prayer of getting into this lot on his own, and Sally will be up to her eyes. She's organising the ball. Come down and find us—if you go down the back stairs by the kitchen, then turn left, you'll see the door to their wing in front of you. Just bang on the door and come in when you're done.'

Libby nodded, and he went out and shut the door, pausing

for a moment to suck in a deep breath before striding along the corridor and down to the communicating door.

He rapped sharply and went in, to find his brother upstairs in the bedroom struggling to attach the starched shirt collar.

'Here, let me,' he said, taking over. 'They're an utter pain in the butt. I just got Libby to dress me. Damn Mum and her grand ideas.'

Will laughed and relinquished the task, lounging against the wall and watching thoughtfully. 'So—had a good day with Libby?'

'Lovely,' he said tightly, trying not to think about it. 'Right, put this on and let's try and do the front studs,' he said, holding out the shirt, and Will shrugged into it and stood while he struggled with the fastenings. 'Cock-eyed, antiquated arrangement,' he grumbled, then stood back. 'Bow-tie?'

'I can do that. Have a drink—there's a nice malt in the kitchen.'

'No. I might have to shoot off.'

'You can't!'

'There's a boy in PICU—'

'When isn't there? Ring and find out how he's doing. Then you can relax.'

'Never that straightforward, though, is it?' he murmured, keying in the number and checking on his little patient.

'Well?'

'He's stable. No change—which is good. I'm hopeful.'

'Excellent. So get yourself a drink and tell me all about Libby while I do this blasted tie up.'

# CHAPTER FOUR

SHE stared at herself in the mirror.

It was a fabulous dress, she had to agree with Amy, but the cleavage worried her and she was concerned about the formality of the occasion. Was flesh allowed? Because there was plenty of it.

She groaned and gave the top another little tug. If only Andrew was here and she could show it to him before she walked through the house and made an utter fool of herself, but of course he wasn't, and he wasn't going to be, so she shrugged, draped the oyster pink pashmina around her shoulders and flipped the end back over her left shoulder so it covered her chest, and then studied her reflection again.

Better. More—well, less, really. She wriggled into the shoes, turned sideways for one last check for VPL, then took a deep breath and opened the door, to find Andrew on the other side, his hand poised to knock.

'Ah—you're ready,' he said, his eyes scanning her. 'I was just coming to check you were OK.'

'Yes—well, I think so. Will I do? Formal enough?'

He opened his mouth, shut it as if he'd thought better of whatever he was going to say and nodded. 'Perfect,' he said, but she wasn't convinced. What had he been going to say?

'Is there a subtext—like, no flesh showing or anything?' she asked, still unsure because of course he couldn't see the neckline with the pashmina in the way, but he just gave a slightly strained laugh and shook his head.

'No, flesh is fine. I've just seen Charlie in the hall, with a dress slit up virtually to the waist, so unless there really isn't a front to that dress under the shawl thing, I don't think you've got a problem. You'll have to go a long way to show more than her.'

She felt her shoulders drop with relief, and the pashmina slid down and his eyes tracked its path, stopping at her cleavage, and they both froze.

She swallowed hard. 'Still think it's all right?' she asked, her nerves on edge for some reason, and after an endless moment he reached for the pashmina and tucked it back over her left shoulder again with gentle fingers.

'On second thoughts, perhaps a little decorum. I don't want my father having a heart attack,' he said gruffly, and then offered her his arm. 'Shall we?'

Damn. She'd known it was too much. Oh, well, it was too late now, but at least she could keep the dress covered. They reached the hall, and Sally came quickly over to them. 'Libby—I've got a corsage for you,' she said, handing her a delicate creamy-white orchid spray, and then she smiled brightly and hurried off.

'I could pin the pashmina with it,' she suggested, and he nodded, looking relieved.

'Good idea. Here, let me.' And he pinned it in place, giving her a fleeting, enigmatic smile, then tucked her hand back in his arm and led her into the fray.

'Oh, my goodness, there are so many people,' she murmured, and he squeezed her hand.

'Don't worry, I won't abandon you,' he promised, and

he didn't. He kept her close all evening, and she was astonished to discover that she was seated next to him at the top table.

If she was supposed to be some kind of deflector for the single girls, she couldn't have been given a more high-profile position, she realised, feeling Charlotte's eyes on her, and she felt the most appalling fraud. The cutlery conundrum came back to haunt her, and if she'd thought that last night's dinner was formal, this was even more so.

But she coped, somehow, managing the endless selection of knives and forks and spoons by following Andrew's lead, making polite conversation to his uncle on her other side and hoping that she wouldn't knock over her wine glass or drop something down the pashmina so she had to take it off and reveal all.

But she got through the meal without a disaster, and then his father tapped a glass and stood up.

'Friends, family, may I have your attention? As you all know, we're here to celebrate Jane's birthday, and I just wanted to say a very few words in praise of a woman who's been a remarkable wife and companion to me for nearly thirty-five years—forty, if you count the time I spent chasing after her before she let me catch her,' he said to a ripple of laughter. 'And I'd be lying if I said she didn't look a day older than on her twenty-first birthday, but she's certainly no less beautiful, at least to me, and I would just like to thank her, in front of you all, for the many years of happiness she's brought me, for the laughter and tears, the companionship, the challenge, and most particularly for the precious gift of our two sons. I know they would like a chance to thank her publicly for all she's done, so if you could bear with us—Andrew? Would you like to start?'

He'd known it was coming, but he'd managed to ignore

it, so preoccupied by the earlier glimpse of Libby's cleavage that his brain had been all but wiped clean. He got to his feet and smiled at everyone, then looked up the table to his mother, ignoring the hastily scribbled notes in his pocket and deciding to wing it. This was his mother, after all. If he couldn't tell her what he thought of her without notes, it was a pretty poor thing.

'You had no idea what you started thirty-four years ago, did you, Mum?' he teased. 'Well, let me tell you. You made me curious. You made me want to know the answers, to persevere until I got them, to change the way it was if I didn't like what I learned, and to live with what I couldn't change. You taught me never to give up, never to give in, never to walk away from anything except a fight. You taught me the difference between right and wrong, the difference between pride and arrogance. You taught me to walk, to ride, to swim, to laugh at myself and not others, to read all sorts of fascinating and amazing things—and to love. You taught me not only to work, but also to play, the value of family, the importance of caring.

'You're a remarkable woman, and you've made me what I am; I owe it all to you, so thank you for that, from the bottom of my heart.'

He sat down again, a lump in his throat, and felt Libby's hand squeeze his under the table before she turned towards Will. He was on his feet, and as they all waited for him to speak, the applause died away until the silence in the room was deafening.

Libby swallowed and bit her lip, her hand still in Andrew's, her eyes fixed on his brother. For the first time, Will wasn't smiling, and she felt her heart miss a beat.

'Well, what can I say?' he began eventually. 'I do public speaking all the time as part of my fundraising work, but this isn't public, this is my mother, the woman who gave birth to me, who taught me all the things she taught Andrew—and, technically, she's entitled to her pension now, but there's no way I'm going to let her retire from the fray without a fight,' he said, smiling briefly at the ripple of laughter through the room. But then his smile faded and he carried on.

'She had no idea when she had us, as Andrew said, what she was letting herself in for. I'm sure we were vile to bring up. Two healthy young boys, hell bent on living as fast and as hard as possible, but then it all got a little more serious, and without Ma's quick thinking I know I wouldn't be here today, so I cannot—*cannot*—underestimate what she means to me, and to the charities for which she works so tirelessly.

'It's because of her,' he concluded, 'that I'm able to stand here in front of you today on my own two feet, to thank her, and to ask you to join with me in raising a glass to her and wishing her a very happy birthday. Happy birthday, Ma. And thank you.'

Everyone got to their feet, the applause thunderous as Will turned to his mother and hugged her hard, then sat down, his eyes over-bright.

She glanced up at Andrew and realised he wasn't doing much better as he turned to her and held the chair for her to sit down again.

'You OK?' she murmured, and he smiled wryly and nodded.

'Yeah, I'm fine. It's just—he never talks about it like that. Not so openly, not to her. And it's—'

'Ladies and gentlemen, could I have your attention, please?'

Sally was on her feet now, standing beside Will with an

envelope in her hand, and she looked round at everyone, then continued as silence fell, 'Her sons don't know this, but Lady Ashenden asked not to receive any presents for her birthday. As she put it, "What on earth could a woman of my age possibly need that I haven't already got?" And so, at her suggestion, anyone who felt that they would like to commemorate her birthday in this way was invited to make a donation to the charities they support for meningitis research and meningococcal disease, and I have to say you've been amazingly generous, because the total at the moment, not counting several last-minute donations, stands at twenty-seven thousand, six hundred and forty-five pounds.'

Will's jaw sagged, and beside Libby, Andrew sucked in his breath.

He looked across at Will, realised he was beyond saying anything and got to his feet again, holding his hands up for silence. 'I don't know what to say,' he began when the cheers and clapping had died away. 'Thank you, obviously. Thank you all so very, very much. The difference your generosity and the generosity of others like you all over the country makes to the children reached by these charities is immeasurable, and for them, for all the children who through donations like this one achieve a greater measure of independence and self-belief, we would all like to give you our heartfelt thanks. And, Mum, I guess we owe you lunch.'

That brought laughter to a room filled with too much emotion, and moments later a huge birthday cake was wheeled in, blazing with candles, and they all—him, his brother, his father—had to go with her to blow the candles out.

Lady Ashenden, near to tears but quietly dignified, thanked all her guests—for coming, for their enormous generosity—and then put her arms around both of her sons and hugged them hard.

For Libby, sitting alone now on the top table, the whole event was deeply moving, and she felt incredibly privileged to have been invited. Will's story had had a happy ending, but it wasn't always like that. She'd seen it happen, seen the devastation caused by the disease. Not many. It wasn't that common, but you never forgot the children you'd worked with in that situation, and even one was too many.

Surreptitiously she wiped away her tears, sniffed hard and drained her wine glass.

'Bit of a tear-jerker, isn't it?'

She looked at Sally, who'd perched on Andrew's chair beside her, and dredged up a smile. 'Yes. How did you manage to speak to everyone after that? I would have been in bits. I *was* in bits.'

She shrugged. 'I've heard him speak before, and it's always very powerful. That's how he's so effective at fund-raising. He does it every time—but this time, it was about his mother, and, well, to be honest I nearly didn't make it! Still, it's over now. They'll bring the cake round, and she's going to circulate while we all have coffee and eat the cake, then it's dancing! And Will says you've promised him a dance, so don't forget.'

Libby laughed. 'Yes—he says he's a better dancer than Andrew, and I have to check it out.'

'Does he, indeed? We'll see about that,' Andrew murmured from behind her, and she felt his hands settle warmly on her shoulders and pull her back against him. She tilted her head back to smile at him, and he dropped a kiss lightly on her forehead. She'd been about to reply, but the words dried up instantly and she forgot her own name as he scooped her up and sat down, settling her back on his lap with his arms looped round her waist.

Instinctively she put her arm around his shoulders to steady herself, her hand splayed over his shoulder, feeling the play of muscle beneath her fingertips through the fine wool of his tailcoat. She could feel the warmth from his muscular legs seeping through her dress, the solid bulk of his chest against her side, and the fact that they were doing it all for Cousin Charlotte's benefit seemed neither here nor there.

Her heart skittering in her chest, she ate her cake perched on his lap, sipped her coffee, laughed with them all when Will came over and cracked an endless succession of dreadful jokes, and then finally it was time to dance. The doors through to the ballroom were rolled aside, the music started and Andrew patted her on the bottom.

'Up you get, it's time to go and check out Will's theory,' he said, his eyes challenging his brother's, and her heart, which had only just settled, lurched against her ribs. She realised she'd been waiting for this since Will had issued the challenge the night before, and at last she was going to know what it was like to be held in Andrew's arms.

There was no question in her mind who would win. Will was fabulous—funny, sexy, outrageous—but he did nothing for her. Andrew, on the other hand…

The four of them headed to the dance floor in time to see Lord and Lady Ashenden have the first dance, and when Libby saw the string quartet, she felt a bubble of delighted laughter rise in her throat.

'Oh, proper dancing!' she said softly, enchanted.

He grinned. 'Well, we can make it improper if you like, but it's a little public.'

She punched his arm lightly and laughed, trying to ignore the little shiver of anticipation. 'You know what I mean. I just haven't ever done it except at dance classes. I didn't think people still did except on television.'

'Only sometimes. And one of the advantages of a stuffy, classical education is that I'm unlikely to step on your toes too often,' he said with a wry smile, and held out his hand to her, sketching a mocking bow as his eyes sparkled with challenge. 'So, shall we show my brother what we're made of?'

He'd been aching to hold her in his arms all night, longing for the moment to come, and he discovered to his delight that she was a beautiful, natural dancer. She followed his lead without a hitch, her hand light on his shoulder, her body just a fraction too far away for his liking—but that was probably just as well, given the total lack of privacy.

And when the time came he was reluctant in the extreme to hand her over to Will.

'She's lovely,' Sally said, smiling up at him as he led her to the side of the dance floor and settled her into a chair so that she could rest. 'A real sweetheart. I'm so glad you've found her.'

'Don't jump the gun,' he warned. 'She's just a friend.'

'Of course she is,' Sally said calmly. 'She's pretty, though. Delightful. And very intelligent. Will likes her a lot.'

'I can see that,' he growled, watching his laughing brother and the woman who was supposed to be his girlfriend twirling past in a flutter of shimmering silk and coat tails. Damn him, if he held her any closer...

'It's about time you found somebody nice,' Sally murmured, and he grunted. If only, he thought.

If only...

'So who's better?'

Torn by loyalty and honesty and a dislike of conflict of any sort, Libby looked from one brother to the other, and shook her head. 'Technically, I don't have the expertise to choose between you, so I would say you're quits. Andrew's very easy to follow, and Will might have the edge when it comes to fancy moves. You're both extremely good, and neither of you trod on my toes, which rates an A star in my book.'

'Very prettily put, but you didn't answer the question,' Will said, grinning. 'I knew you wouldn't.'

'Equal first?' she offered. 'I can't choose between you.'

'Or won't.'

'Oh, Libby, just tell him he's better,' Andrew groaned. 'Let him win. He won't give up until you do. It's not worth it.'

'OK, he's better. Is that what you want to hear?'

'Yes!' Will said smugly, and punched the air.

Andrew rolled his eyes and sighed. 'He's going to be insufferable. Take him away, Sally.'

'Good idea,' Sally said, hoisting herself out of the chair and rubbing her back. 'It's past my bedtime and it's certainly past his.'

'Oh, promises,' Will murmured with a grin, and he slung his arm round Sally's shoulders, winked at them and steered her towards the door, looking slightly the worse for wear.

'So, who *is* better?' Andrew asked softly, wondering what she'd say now they were alone, and she turned and met his eyes.

'I don't know. I think I need to check a few things out again,' she said deadpan.

His mouth quirked in a fleeting smile, and he held out his hand. 'Check away,' he murmured, drawing her into his arms and easing her closer.

The tempo had slowed, and he rested his cheek against her hair and breathed in the curiously intoxicating scent of apples. Her body settled gently against his, so he felt the soft press of her breasts against his chest, the light brush of her thighs, the curve of her waist under his hand.

He could feel himself responding, felt her breath catch, then ease out again as she settled yet closer, and suddenly he couldn't take it any more. He was too tired to control his reaction, too tired to fight the need to hold her; the lack of sleep was beginning to catch up with him, and he didn't count the few hours he'd spent trying not to fall off the miserable excuse for a bed in the dressing room, so he forced himself to ease away and meet her eyes. 'To be honest, I could call it a night, Libby, unless you want to stay up? I'm bushed.'

'I'm more than happy to give up. These shoes are killing me,' she murmured. Her eyes were soft, luminous, and he wasn't sure if she'd misunderstood his intentions. He hoped not. He really had meant it when he had said no strings.

They made their way upstairs, and at the bedroom door he hesitated. He couldn't go in there with her—not now. Not yet. He couldn't trust himself while his arms still held the memory of her body swaying against him for dance after dance after dance. 'I just want to say goodnight to my parents,' he said a little desperately. 'I need to head off in the morning early and we probably won't see them before we go. Don't wait up for me.'

And turning on his heel he left her there, walking swiftly away before he gave in to the temptation to usher her through the door, strip off that dress that only he had seen the top of, and make love to her until neither of them could move another muscle.

So that was her told.

Don't wait up for me, indeed. Of course not. Why would she? After all, she wasn't really his girlfriend, and she'd done her job now, fended off the girls all evening, smiled and laughed through one dance after another in his arms so he didn't have to dance with them.

Show only, just a smokescreen, a deflector for the poor, love-lorn Charlotte and her cohorts, Libby thought wearily, and unpinning the orchid from her shoulder and removing the shawl, she peeled off the dress, pulled on her nightdress and took off her make-up, cleaned her teeth and slid into the chilly bed.

It would have been nice if he'd been in it with her, she thought, and then laughed softly to herself. Nice? There would have been nothing nice about it, it would have been amazing. Incredible. And utterly not going to happen.

She turned over so her back was to the door, and waited for him. She'd turned out the light in her room, leaving on the dressing-room light so he could see, and lay there in the semi-darkness waiting for his return, knowing that when he came back to the room he'd expect to find her sleeping, but she couldn't sleep, for some reason. Not until he was back.

Eventually she heard him moving quietly around, heard the click of the switch as the light went out and the room settled into darkness, and then at last, exhausted, she drifted off to sleep...

It was pitch-dark when she woke.

She could hear him moving around, and she sat up and peered towards the noise.

'Andrew?'

'Oh, Libby, I'm sorry, I didn't mean to wake you. I was going to get a drink from the kitchen.'

'I could do with one, too. Can I come with you?'

'Sure. We can make a cup of tea, if you like.'

She turned on her bedside light and then regretted it instantly, because he was wearing a pair of loose cotton scrub trousers and nothing else. They hung low on his hips, showing the taut, firm abdomen, the broad, deep chest and wide shoulders she'd found so fascinating the previous morning when he'd emerged from the shower in his towel, but that had been before she'd danced with him, before she'd felt that solid, muscular body against hers, felt his masculine response, and she felt her tongue dry up and stick to the roof of her mouth.

'Did you steal them from the hospital?' she asked, raising a brow at the impromptu PJs and trying to remember how to breathe, and he chuckled.

'No, they're from college. I found them in the drawer. I don't—ah…'

He trailed off, and she felt warmth brush her cheeks. He didn't—what? Wear anything usually? She closed her eyes for a second and turned back the bedclothes, tugging her nightdress down over her legs even though it was more than respectable, and trying very hard not to think about him wearing nothing.

'Do you have a dressing gown?' he asked, and when she shook her head, he handed her the one off the back of the door and pulled on the jumper he'd been wearing the previous day. Better, but not much, she thought, the image of him burned on her retinas.

She shrugged into the dressing gown and realised instantly it was his. His scent was on it, her warmth releasing a heady mixture of his signature cologne and that subtle masculine essence that was his alone. It was like having him wrapped around her, holding her close, she thought, and her heart picked up speed.

She followed him through the house, along the dark corridor and down the stairs to the warm, cosy kitchen where they'd had breakfast the previous morning. The dogs greeted them sleepily, and Andrew sat her down at the table and put the kettle on the Aga, then pulled out another chair and stretched out his legs towards the warmth, tipping his head back and closing his eyes.

'Bliss. I love the house when everyone's asleep,' he murmured.

'I get the feeling that being awake at night is a habit for you, or am I wrong?'

He shrugged. 'No, you're not wrong. I don't tend to sleep well. Too busy, I suppose. I just felt thirsty, and my mind was working.'

'Jacob?'

He opened his eyes and levered himself upright again. 'No. Well, a bit, but mostly family stuff. I was thinking about Mum, about all she's done over the years.'

About how she'd put him in the same room as Libby and left him to die of frustration…

The kettle boiled and he got to his feet and made them tea—green tea for him, chamomile for Libby, so they weren't awake for the rest of the night—then leant over Libby to put her cup down and got another drift of apples from her hair.

Damn, he was going to embarrass himself at this rate, he thought, and turning the chair so he was facing the table, he sat down and propped his elbows on the scrubbed pine surface and sipped his tea until he was back under control.

They didn't talk, just sat in a comfortable silence as they had over their picnic, and drank their tea until it was finished. And then the tension, suddenly, was back.

'I suppose we ought to get some more sleep,' she said eventually, and he nodded.

'Yes, we probably should.'

They went back up to his room, the tension somehow

ratcheting up with every step, and as they reached the door Libby's heart was in her mouth. Would he kiss her? No. Why would he?

But he hesitated, closing the door and standing there, his eyes locked with hers, and she could see the need in them.

'Andrew?' she said softly, his name an invitation, should he choose to accept it, but he closed his eyes fleetingly.

'Libby, no,' he murmured. 'I promised you—'

'I won't hold you to it.'

He shook his head. 'I can't—Libby, there are all sorts of reasons.'

'Such as? Are you married and I don't know?'

He laughed at that, the sound soft, a little raw. 'No, I'm not married.'

'Then stay with me. Please?'

'Libby, I—' Oh, God, she didn't know what she was asking of him. He saw the uncertainty in her eyes, knew how much it had taken for her to ask him, and he couldn't do it, couldn't leave her, couldn't turn away from her in that moment no matter how stupid it was to stay. How dangerous.

He held out his arms to her, and she went into them, warm and soft and yielding, and he felt heat sear through him. 'Libby—'

Her lips found his, gentle at first, tentative, but then when he gave up fighting it and started to kiss her back she gave a little sob and arched against him, and he cradled her face in his hands and deepened the kiss, ravaging her mouth, tasting the sweetness, the satin softness, searching out the hot, honeyed depths, their tongues tangling as they duelled. Her legs parted to the pressure of his thigh, and he rocked against her, aching for her, needing her, needing to bury himself inside her and take the treasure she was offering.

His hand left her face, feathering down over her throat,

tracing the pulse that hammered beneath his fingertips, down over her collar bone, over the satin-soft skin of her chest until it reached the warm, enticing swell of her breast. The nightdress was in the way, tangled round her legs, hampering his hand at her breast, and he pushed himself away, stripping back the bedclothes, peeling off his sweater and reaching for her, easing the dressing gown aside so it slid down her arms and puddled on the floor behind her.

She held up her arms, her eyes locked with his, and with a tiny hiss of breath he reached for the hem of her nightdress and stripped it off her.

He heard it rip, but he didn't care. He was beyond caring, beyond anything except making the woman standing there beside him his. He tugged at the cord on his scrubs, the knot releasing so they fell to the floor with his dressing gown and the torn nightdress as he stood there drinking her in with his gaze. Her eyes were wide and liquid, her mouth softly swollen, her breasts full and yet yielding, perfect, the dusky rose nipples tightly pebbled and so, so tempting. He lowered his head, taking one in his mouth, drawing it in, suckling on her deeply as she arched against him, crying out.

'Andrew, please!'

His hand moved on, down over the smooth plane of her flank, across her hip, over the bowl of her pelvis, on again.

She bucked against him, her legs jerking as his hand found her, found the secret, hidden depths, the moist heat of her most intimate places. His thumb grazed her and her eyes flew wide, her breath catching, and suddenly he couldn't wait another moment.

Scooping her up in his arms, he laid her gently on the bed, his eyes still fixed on hers, their breath mingling as he moved over her and entered her with one long, slow stroke, driving her over the edge, her body convulsing around him, her cries dragging him after her to join her in the wild tumult of their release...

She woke for the second morning in a row to the sound of running water, and she lay and pictured him in the shower. She could do it better today, could see his body, knew it, every inch.

Beautiful. Magnificent. Solidly powerful, lean and graceful, potent.

Oh, lord.

She heard the water stop, then gave him a moment and tapped on the door, tugging her ripped nightdress into place. 'Are you decent? Can I come in?'

'Yeah, sure.'

She opened the door and sucked in her breath. 'Oh! Sorry—I thought—'

His mouth twisted into a wry, teasing smile and he lowered the towel from his hair. 'I've just made love to you, Libby,' he murmured softly. 'Exactly which bit of me do you want covered up?'

She felt the heat in her cheeks, but she held her ground and dragged her eyes from his body. 'Actually, that was the thing I wanted to talk to you about. Last night, when we— you didn't use—I'm not on the Pill,' she muttered, floundering to an embarrassed halt.

He put the towel he was holding in one hand back on the towel rail and let out a long, thoughtful sigh. 'Well, I don't think it's an issue—not for you, at any rate. I—ah...' He hesitated, gave a low laugh and met her eyes, his own carefully blank. 'I can't get you pregnant.'

'What—? Why not?'

'Because I'm infertile,' he said quietly.

She felt her mouth drop open with shock, and shut it with a little snap. 'How do you know?'

He gave a little grunt of laughter. 'Oh, we were messing about at college,' he said with forced lightness. 'You know what it's like—well, no, to be fair, you probably don't, you're not a boy, but we had one of these stupid ideas that we'd become sperm donors. Loads of medical students do it, and we decided it was no hardship—and there we were, in the lab without a lecturer, all these microscopes lying about, and someone decided while we were on the subject that it would be funny to see who'd got the highest sperm count. And I didn't have any. Well, a few, swimming in circles, whereas they had millions all thrashing away and swimming like hell.'

She sagged against the wall, hugging her arms around her torn nightdress, staring at him blankly, trying to imagine what it had been like for this young man in the prime of his life to find out something so devastating. 'So—what did they say? Your friends?'

'Nothing. They didn't know. I accidentally contaminated my sample from someone else's Petri dish—not very honest, but I was reeling, really. I needed time to take it in, and I certainly wasn't ready to go public with that lot.'

'Oh, Andrew,' she said softly, her heart aching for him. 'That must have been awful.'

His mouth tugged down at one side. 'It was. But then I thought, later that day when I'd calmed down a bit and it had sunk in, I'd had glandular fever after I started uni, I'd had mumps really badly at seventeen, and Will had only just been discharged from hospital. It had been a comprehensively bloody four years, what with one thing and another, and I thought, well, it's just temporary. It'll recover. But it didn't.'

'You got it tested properly?'

He shook his head. 'What's to test? Either they're there, swimming, or they're not. I managed to wangle my way out of the sperm donor thing and checked again, a few weeks later. Then periodically until eventually I gave up. It seemed pointless, going on, there's a limit to how often you want to remind yourself of something like that.'

'And you've never got anybody pregnant?'

'I've never had unprotected sex before last night,' he said softly, then breaking eye contact at last, he turned back to the basin and started to shave, and she watched him for a moment, let his words play through her head, and she felt warmth flood her body—warmth, at his gentle admission of this new intimacy, and then, perversely, regret that it could have no consequences. And relief, because there was no way she could afford to get accidentally pregnant.

Not yet, at least. Not until she knew…

# CHAPTER FIVE

SHE left him to it, going back to the bedroom and sitting on the bed, staring at the rumpled sheets where she'd lain in his arms all night.

Infertile.

She shook her head, struggling to take it in, and then lifted her case and put it on the bed and started to pack. She found clean underwear, packed all the things she didn't need, then when he was out of the bathroom she showered quickly, wrapped her hair in a towel and packed her wash things.

She knew he wanted to get away promptly this morning, the condition of the child in PICU worrying away at him even though he hadn't admitted it last night, and anyway she had to get back to feed the cat.

She was glad they were leaving early before anyone else would be about. She was still feeling the shock of his revelation all the way down to her toes, and she was sure it would show in her eyes—quite apart from the whisker burn on her top lip and the softness around her eyes, a dead giveaway of how they'd spent the night. And sitting with his family over breakfast while they sized her up as potential material for a daughter-in-law and mother of the future Lord Ashenden would be too much. His poor parents were so desperate for him to give them grandchildren, and the fact that Sally was pregnant didn't alter that.

His parents, Jane especially, wanted him settled with a wife and children; she'd gathered that much from the odd hint and joke over the course of the weekend, and now she knew the truth, her heart ached for him. No wonder he hadn't wanted to come home for the house party! It was a miracle he ever came home at all.

'Leave your case on the bed, I'll come up and get it in a minute. I'm going to make tea,' he called through the door.

'Don't worry, take it now,' she said, coming out of the bathroom in a towel and throwing her wash bag and night-dress into the top of the case and zipping it shut. 'I've got everything I need.'

Everything except him, but that was never going to happen. She reached for his arm, meeting his eyes, seeing the pain still echoed there, dragged back to life by their conversation.

'Andrew, I'm so sorry.'

'Don't be. It doesn't matter.'

'You don't want children?'

His smile was sad. 'I'm a paediatrician, Libby. What do you think? But we don't always get what we want, and I have a fulfilling and very rewarding life. Besides, I'm still single. And I don't need children to make me happy.'

'But your mother does. She's desperate for you to settle down—and it's why you're still single, isn't it? Does she even know?'

He shook his head. 'No. And she doesn't need to know. Nobody knows.'

'Not even Will?'

He gave a short laugh. 'Especially not Will.'

So he didn't even have his brother's comfort or support.

'Ah, Libby, no, don't cry for me,' he said softly, and drew her into his arms. 'Hush now, come on. It's all right, truly. I'm OK. And I'll marry one day, someone who's already got children so she doesn't feel tempted to leave me because there's something missing in her life.'

'Do you really think all women are that shallow?' she demanded, but he just laughed softly.

'No. Not shallow, not at all. But the drive to procreate is a strong one, and I wouldn't ask any woman to give up her right to be a mother. It wouldn't be fair.'

'And what about you, Andrew? What about what's fair to you?'

He didn't answer, just turned away after a moment, picked up her case and left the room.

They were gone half an hour later, without disturbing anyone. He'd already said goodbye to his parents the night before, and he'd ring Will later. He'd understand—and, anyway, he was probably still in bed with Sally, sleeping off his excesses, or else he'd be out riding.

'I need to go straight to the hospital. Is it OK if I just drop you off and shoot away?' he asked, and she nodded.

'Of course it is. Anyway, I've got things to do.'

'Laundry?' he suggested, his smile wry.

She laughed. 'You guessed it. And dusting. And vacuuming up the drifts of cat hair.'

He pulled up outside her little modern terraced house and cut the engine, then lifted her case out of the boot and put it down in her hall. 'Thank you for coming with me,' he said softly. 'And I'm sorry—it really wasn't meant to end up the way it did. I shouldn't have taken advantage of you last night.'

'Excuse me?' Her mouth kicked up in a smile that unravelled something deep in his gut. 'I don't remember you taking advantage—if anyone did, it was me. I seem to remember I kissed you first.'

'OK,' he said at last, giving her a fleeting smile. 'I'll give you that. But—Libby, I meant what I said. I'm not in the market for a serious relationship. I don't want to hurt you, and I don't want to get hurt myself, and I think it might be all too easy to fall into a relationship that hurts us both in the end.'

Her eyes clouded, and she gave a slight nod and stepped back. 'That's OK. I understand. We're just friends. Not even that, really. Colleagues. We'll just pretend it never happened.'

He nodded, kissed her cheek and left her there, getting back into the car and driving away, his eyes on the rear-view mirror until he couldn't see her house any longer.

Colleagues. What a curiously unpalatable thought.

'Oh, Kitty, how could I be so stupid? I've gone and fallen in love with him,' she told the cat. Scooping her up, she sat down on the sofa and tried to cuddle her, but the cat was hungry and not having any of it, so she fed her, unpacked her suitcase and hung up Amy's dress.

The pashmina was crumpled, but she put it on a hanger and sorted out her washing, started the first load off and then emptied the dishwasher, cleaned the kitchen and got the vacuum cleaner out. She'd be fine if she kept busy, she told herself, but then she realised she couldn't see, so she gave up, had a howl, blew her nose and made a cup of tea and went to phone Amy.

She'd be gagging to know how it had gone, but she'd only get a very edited version of the truth, and she could always talk about Will. Amy would be fascinated.

Except Amy wasn't there. Amy was obviously out having

some fun of her own, and so Libby put the phone back in the cradle and flicked through the television channels.

Nothing. There was never anything on, and in the middle of a Sunday there was hardly going to be anything riveting. A film she'd seen dozens of times, some sheepdog trials—she threw the remote control down in disgust and went out to the kitchen, dragged the washing out of the machine, loaded it with the next lot and carried the pile of wet clothes upstairs to hang in her bathroom—because, of course, today it was raining.

April showers, torrents of rain falling like stair-rods, hammering on the windows and bouncing off the roof of her little conservatory. Nothing would dry outside today, and precious little would dry inside. And she'd let it drift for too long.

Oh, damn, she thought, and decided to have a bath. A nice long, hot soak, a cup of tea and a book. And who cared if it was the middle of the day?


'How's he been?'

'Good.' The PICU charge nurse talked him through the charts, and he went and spoke to the parents—exhausted, drained, but still fighting—and bent over the bed with a smile.

'Hi, Jacob. How are you doing?' he asked, although the boy was unconscious and on a ventilator. 'I'm just going to have a look at you, see what's going on here.'

He scanned the monitors, examined the damaged limbs for swelling, checked the pulse in his feet and nodded. 'His legs and pelvis are looking good,' he said to the parents.

'Do you think so?' Jacob's mother Tracy said, hope in her voice. 'We can't really tell, but his toes are nice and pink and he's been—I don't know, quieter, somehow. More as if he's resting, more comfortable.'

He felt the tension ease a fraction. Not completely, he would never become complacent, but Jacob seemed more stable.

'He's making progress. I'm happier with him than I was before the weekend, and I think we'll get a good result.'

Then he headed to the ward and had a chat to the boys, checked with the nursing staff that they had no problems or queries and then left the ward, hurrying to get back out into the fresh air again, restless and uncertain about how to fill the rest of the day.

Which was absurd, because he had a mountain of paperwork to deal with on his desk at home, his laundry was in no better a situation than Libby's—although to be fair that was because he hadn't got round to dropping it into the dry cleaner's for them to deal with—and he ought to go to the supermarket before it shut at four.

He'd do that first.

He must be crazy.

Andrew sat at the end of Libby's little cul-de-sac and stared at her house pensively. He'd told her the situation, told her he didn't want a relationship, and he didn't, he really didn't, so why the hell was he here, hovering outside like some kind of bloody stalker?

But he wanted her. Wanted to see her, wanted to talk to her, wanted to hold her. He could take her out to dinner, bring her back, leave her at the door. He didn't have to make love to her—

Who was he kidding? His body was getting hard just thinking about her. And she knew the score. And she, as she'd pointed out, had been the one who'd made the first move. She'd reached for him.

And even if it had only been a split second before he

would have reached for her, nevertheless, she *had* made the first move.

But she hadn't known the truth then. If she had, would it have made a difference? He'd never know. And he had bags full of food that needed to go in the fridge. He'd taken enough of her time.

And then her front door opened and she came out, dressed in jeans and a thick cream jumper with a binbag in her hand, and she looked up and saw him and stopped in her tracks.

He got out of the car and walked over to her slowly, and her eyes searched his face.

'What? What is it? Not the kid in PICU?'

He shook his head. 'No. He's looking better—well, slightly. I just—I've been to the supermarket, and I was virtually passing, and—'

He scrubbed a hand round the back of his neck, then smiled at her, and Libby felt her heart turn over. 'I know I said a load of stuff this morning about not having relationships, but—are you busy?'

She felt herself smile before she could control it, and shook her head. 'No, Andrew, I'm not busy. Come in. Have you got anything that needs to be in the fridge?'

He shook his head. 'It'll keep. It's not exactly hot out here, and the temperature's starting to drop already. It'll be fine—ah. Except for the ice cream.'

'You bought ice cream? What sort?'

'Belgian chocolate. Is there any other sort?'

She laughed. 'You'd better bring it in, but don't blame me if you don't get to take it home.' And dumping the binbag in her wheelie bin, she went back into the house and left him to follow.

'Oh. You've brought a bag. Does that all need the freezer?'

He shook his head. 'No. It's the bag with the ice cream in it, but I've got other things in here—things I was going to cook tonight. I just wondered, if you really aren't busy, if you'd let me cook for you. But if you are, just tell me to take a hike.'

'I'm not busy,' she said, taking the bag out of his hand, extracting the ice cream and putting it in the freezer, then putting the bag in the fridge. 'Tea?'

'Lovely. I haven't had a drink for hours.'

'Neither have I. I've been in the bath and I fell asleep.'

Oh, hell, he thought. Why had she told him that? Now all he could see was her beautiful, curvy body lapped by warm water, and desire, hot, hard and far from slaked by last night's all too brief interlude, came screaming back to life.

This was such a profoundly lousy idea, he thought, but then she put the kettle on and turned towards him, propped herself against the worktop and smiled a rueful smile and he thought, She feels the same. She wasn't going to do this, but she wants to just as much as I do.

And there was no way he could walk away.

Libby studied him for a long moment. There was a muscle working in his jaw, and she could see the throb of his pulse just above the unbuttoned collar of his shirt. She reached into the cupboard above the kettle, took out two glasses and filled them with water, handing him one.

He tilted his head in puzzlement, taking it from her and lifting it to his lips.

'You didn't really want to wait for tea, did you?' she murmured, and he choked on the water.

Laughing helplessly, she took the glass out of his hand and slapped him on the back, then as he straightened, eyes streaming, his mouth curved with self-deprecating humour, she slipped her hand into his and led him out of the kitchen, through the living room and up the stairs. By the time she turned to face him, they were standing by her bed and all trace of the smile was gone, replaced by a burning urgency in his eyes that stole her breath away.

'I think you're trying to kill me,' he said softly as she peeled off the white sweater and dropped it on the floor. She'd kicked off her shoes, unfastened her jeans and started to slide them down her hips before he moved, then he tore his shirt off over his head, buttons pinging in all directions, kicked off his shoes, shucked his trousers, boxers and socks in one movement and eased her slowly up against him.

'Oh, that feels so good,' he muttered, then his mouth found hers and she sighed with relief.

She'd really thought it was over, that they'd go back to being colleagues, that the weekend would be put aside as if it had never happened—but no. He kissed her as if he'd die without her, slanting his head to get a better angle, one hand threaded into her hair, his fingers splayed, cradling her head, the other hand sliding round behind her and cupping her bottom, groaning as he hauled her closer, so she felt the hard jut of his erection against her abdomen.

Then he lifted his head and stared down into her eyes, easing away fractionally, his chest heaving. 'Libby, I—I bought condoms,' he said gruffly. 'I didn't know if you were worried about it—you know, for other reasons.'

She shook her head. 'No. I trust you, and I've always been really careful, so if you don't think it's necessary I don't want anything between us.'

He sucked in his breath and closed his eyes then, still holding her with one arm, he dragged the quilt out of the way with the other hand and tipped her back onto the mattress and followed her down, one solid, hair-strewn leg wedged between hers, his hand finding her breast, cupping it tenderly as he brushed his lips across it with a groan.

'You're gorgeous, do you know that? So much woman…'

She felt the deep, slow tug of his mouth on her nipple, the ache low down intensifying, and she tunnelled her fingers through his hair and held him close, giving herself up to the slow, painstaking and very thorough appraisal he was making of her body with his hands and lips.

Her own hands and lips were busy, too, exploring the fascinating textures of his body, the smooth satin skin over corded muscle and sinew, the ripple of reaction as she stroked teasingly over his abdomen, the coarse silk of his body hair, the taste of salt, the warm, rich scent of musk.

There was no hurry now. No urgency. They both knew where this was going to end, and they were taking their time, savouring every second, every last caress.

But then he lifted his head, staring down into her eyes, his own strangely intense.

'I need you, Libby,' he said softly. 'You have no idea how much I need you.'

She reached up, her hand gentle on his cheek, cradling his jaw, relishing the harsh rasp of his beard against her palm.

Her touch was sweet to him, her smile enough to break his heart.

'I'm here,' she murmured, and for a crazy instant, he thought it sounded like a vow…

Libby went into work the following morning walking on air and with a smile she could do nothing to hide.

At least, not from Amy, who promptly grabbed her arm and dragged her into the office when she came up to the ward just before eight, as Libby finished the drugs round.

'Well? I nearly went crazy yesterday! Why didn't you ring me?'

'I tried—you were engaged, then you were out.'

'I wasn't out—oh, rats, you must have rung when I was in the shower. You should have left a message, I've been on edge all night! So, tell all—was it fantastic?'

'Absolutely,' she said, the smile winning hands down. 'It was amazing. Fabulous. Such a beautiful place, and the food was incredible.'

Amy smiled. 'Great. And Andrew?'

Her brows went up, her head tilted, and Libby sighed inwardly. She might have known she wouldn't get away with it! 'We had a lovely weekend; it was a fabulous party, the dress was perfect, so thank you very much for lending it to me, and I didn't fall out of it, which was a relief! I'll get it cleaned.'

'And Andrew?' she prompted again, and Libby shrugged and tried hard not to look away.

'He was lovely—a perfect gentleman. We had a great time, talked a lot, and I've got to know him a bit better, to understand what motivates him. It'll be very useful for working with him.'

Amy's jaw sagged. 'That's it?'

'That's it,' she lied, determined to keep their private moments just that, but Amy looked sceptical and slightly disgusted.

'You're hopeless! "It'll be very useful for working with him,"' she mimicked, making little quote marks in the air and rolling her eyes. 'I despair of you! You go away with that *hunk* and that's the best you can come up with—good grief, Libby, opportunities like that are wasted on you,' she said, and, turning round, she almost fell over Andrew in the office doorway.

Over her head their eyes met, Libby's bubbling over with laughter, Andrew's slightly stunned. Lifting his hands, he stepped back, smiled and said, 'Morning!' and Amy went scarlet, mumbled something unintelligible and fled.

'What was that about?' he asked softly, frowning after her, and Libby chuckled.

'She was getting a bit too close to the nitty-gritty. I thought—well, I didn't know, but I imagined you didn't want to go public,' she said in a quiet undertone, and he nodded.

'No. Thanks for that. I owe you.'

'No, you don't. I don't want it spread all round the hospital either, and I love Amy to bits but it's so easy to let things slip out and then someone else'll get hold of it and it'll be pinned on the notice-board before we know it.'

'Sounds about right. So she thinks I'm a hunk, does she?' he mused thoughtfully, and then Libby caught the twinkle in his eye and laughed.

'Don't get carried away. She's been trying to fix me up with someone for over a year. Any single half-eligible male in the hospital is a hunk under those circumstances.'

'So who's she been trying to fix you up with?' he asked, and for a moment she wondered if that really had been a flash of jealousy in his eyes.

'Nobody. Anybody,' she said honestly. 'I don't date.'

'Why?'

Her heart thumped. Trust Andrew to get straight to the heart of it, but she wasn't ready to talk about it, and this wasn't the time.

'Oh—this and that,' she said flippantly, but she gave a twisted little smile that tugged at his heartstrings.

'Sounds messy,' he murmured, searching her eyes for clues.

She shrugged, the simple gesture hiding a world of hurt. 'A little bit. Whatever,' she said, injecting artificial brightness into her voice. 'What can I do for you?'

'Nothing. I was just passing, on my way back from clinics, and I thought I'd pop in, say hi.'

'Well, hi,' she said, smiling again with her eyes, the demons apparently banished, put back in their box. 'Not busy today?'

'Oh, I'm always busy, but somehow the lure was irresistible.' Something warm and gentle flickered in his expressive eyes, unravelling her a little. 'In fact, how about lunch?'

'Lunch? That would be lovely, if you've got time. Where? The canteen?'

He pulled a face. 'That doesn't really square with keeping things quiet, does it? I've got a better idea. Why don't I pick up some sandwiches and you come to my office for lunch? I've got a coffee machine in there—you know where it is, don't you?'

She nodded. 'What time?'

'What time can you do? Is one any good?'

'Should be fine.'

'Good. We can always pretend it's work.' And glancing over his shoulder, he pushed the door shut and eased her into his arms, dropping a lingering, tender kiss on her lips. 'Just to keep you going,' he murmured, and then with a mischievous wink, he opened the door and strolled out, hands in his pockets, leaving her heart fluttering and a smile on her face she could do nothing about.

She sucked in a deep breath, gave him a minute to get off the ward and then went out. There was lots she should be doing. Joel needed turning, Lucas probably needed stringing up and the twins were getting bored and needed a change of scenery. A little concentration on something other than Andrew would be good for her, she decided, and finding a nurse to help her, she started work.

# CHAPTER SIX

SHE tapped on Andrew's door and went in at his crisp, decisive 'Yes!'

He looked up and blinked, as if he'd been miles away. 'Is it really one already? Sorry, I've been up to my eyes, I had no idea it was so late.'

He closed the folder, got to his feet and came over to her, pushed the door shut and hugged her. 'Sorry, it's been a bit mad round here. I'll make us coffee—have a look through the sandwiches and choose what you want. I wasn't sure what you'd like.'

While he fiddled with the coffee maker, she stared at the pile of plastic containers on his desk and chuckled, poking them around with her finger so she could read the labels. 'Is that why there are four different sorts?'

'Oh, don't worry, I'll eat them later if we don't finish them.'

She picked out the prawn salad on wholemeal and waggled them at him. 'Can I have these?'

'You can have whatever you want. I like them all. Here, coffee.'

He handed her a mug, pulled up another chair to his desk and sat down beside her, ripping the lid off the chicken tikka sandwich and sinking his teeth into it. 'Ah, that's better. I'm starving. The bread was off, I haven't had breakfast.'

'How can bread be off?'

'You know, blue hairy bits.'

She winced. 'Sounds worse than my fridge.'

'It is. I forgot to buy bread yesterday at the supermarket—something to do with a certain ward sister I couldn't get out of my mind,' he said mildly, but his eyes were teasing and she couldn't help smiling back.

'Is that right?'

'It's right.' He chomped down on the sandwich again, demolishing it in another two bites and starting on the next packet. 'So—good day so far?'

She dusted off her hands and picked up her mug. 'I'd like to say yes, but actually, now you come to mention it, not really. There's someone I'd like to talk to you about. Joel. His spirits are down.'

'I'm not surprised. He's going to be a long time in that halo, and having both arms in plaster isn't good either.'

'No. And he hates having to ask for help with all the personal stuff. I was wondering when we could get him up.'

'Oh, probably soon. I'd like him home in a week or two. He'll need looking after, of course, but it's a case of time now and his fracture's stable. I'll get him X-rayed again and see if we think he's ready to start mobilising. And Lucas, too—we need to think about discharging him soon. He must be driving you mad.'

'He is, bless his heart, but I'll miss him.'

He chuckled. 'Liar. He's a pain.'

'No, he's a good kid. Just a little reckless.'

'Talking of which,' he added slowly, 'are you busy this evening? Will and Sally are staying at mine tonight. She's got an antenatal appointment tomorrow, and they're coming in time for supper. We were going to get a takeaway. Would you like to join us?'

'I wouldn't dream of gatecrashing your evening,' she protested, but he just laughed and leant over and kissed her softly.

'Don't be silly. You won't be gatecrashing. I've been wondering how I could slide off later and come round to your house. You'll just save me the effort of sneaking around.'

She searched his eyes, looking for doubts, and found none. 'He'll know, if he sees us together,' she murmured, and he nodded.

'I know. But I trust him, and while I don't want the entire hospital talking about us, I'm quite happy for my brother to know. And, anyway, I'm pretty sure he already does.'

She smiled. 'Then, thank you, that would be lovely. You'd better give me your address—and directions, because I don't have a sat-nav.'

He laughed softly. 'I'll come and get you. Six-thirty, OK?'

'Fine. I'll look forward to it. What should I wear?'

'Oh, nothing smart. Jeans?'

'Jeans it is,' she said with a relieved smile, and sipped her coffee. 'How's Jacob, by the way? I take it he's no worse, since you haven't mentioned him. Or was it him you were running around after all morning?'

'No, fortunately not, that was just following up after the weekend and doing my clinic. He's doing well. We're really hopeful. I've just come from a multi-disciplinary team meeting in PICU, and they're talking about cutting back on the sedation, see how he does. The swelling on his brain's subsiding and he's looking good.'

'Fantastic. I'll keep my fingers crossed. You'll have to let me know how it goes.' She smiled wryly and got to her feet. 'I'd better get on. I've promised Lucas he can go down to the coffee shop with his mum for lunch, and he's talked about nothing but basketball since you mentioned it, apparently! I feel sorry for Amy. She's going to have to get him up and running again double-quick!'

He chuckled, threw their sandwich wrappers in the bin and dropped another of those teasing, lingering kisses on her lips. 'Talking of which, I have to get on, too. I'll see you later,' he murmured, then with a slow, lazy wink, he opened the door for her, waggled his fingers in farewell and went the other way towards the clinics, whistling softly and leaving her to head back to the ward, her heart singing.

She was seeing him tonight, at his home, with his brother. Going public, albeit in a private sort of way. That had to be good—didn't it? Progress?

She was shocked at how much she hoped so.

He picked her up at six thirty-two, by which time she'd showered, changed and changed again. Twice.

Still just jeans, but different jeans, and the cream jumper she'd had on the night before, but then she went back to the original top, not as warm but prettier. And then changed back again into the jumper, just as the doorbell rang. Pretty be damned. She wasn't going to be cold, and there was a bitter nip to the air this evening, to remind them all that it was only April and frosts were not yet a thing of the past.

'We could always skip supper,' he said, sliding his arms round her and nuzzling her neck. 'You smell gorgeous. Apples and cinnamon—like apple pie.'

She laughed a little breathlessly. 'That's apple shampoo and a spicy scent Amy gave me for Christmas.'

'Good for Amy—nice choice,' he said, releasing her reluctantly and standing back. 'Ready to go? Where's your overnight bag?'

She hesitated. 'Is that a good idea? Then I'll have to rely

on you for transport tomorrow. That's going to be a bit obvious when we arrive for work.'

He nodded. 'You're right.'

'You could always stay here, though,' she suggested tentatively.

'Or you could follow me in your car, with your things. That way we can all see more of each other and I'll have time to talk to Will in the morning. I've got some things I need to discuss with him before I go to work, and I don't need to start tomorrow until eight-thirty, but you can shoot off when you're ready.'

'Oh.' She felt a flicker of doubt. The weekend at his parents' house was one thing. This, inviting her round to join him for the night while Will and Sally were there, was quite another, for a man who'd said he didn't want a relationship. 'Are you sure you want me to come?'

'Absolutely sure. I told you that earlier. Get your things. I'll draw you a map in case you lose me.'

'Don't lose me,' she said, and he smiled as if he understood.

'I won't,' he promised.

She stuck to him like glue.

His first stop was to the Indian takeaway on the corner near the hospital, and then he headed out into the country.

Not far, just a couple of miles, but far enough that they left the lights behind them and turned onto a narrow, winding little lane. He swept onto a gently shelving drive, triggering security lights, and came to a halt in front of a sprawling single-storey barn conversion, and she parked beside him and looked around.

It was impressive, but not overly so—not outrageously ostentatious like Ashenden, just tasteful and well groomed, the gravel free of weeds, the low beds of ground cover neatly tended, the house itself welcoming, with big, heavy pots of clipped bay each side of the entrance, formal and yet understated. She couldn't wait to see the inside.

There was a 4 x 4 on the drive—Will's? Probably.

'Slow enough?' he asked, resting his arm on the top of her door and smiling down at her as she cut the engine.

'Perfect. Is that Will's car?'

He nodded. 'They've been here a while. Come on in.'

He opened the door, and Lara bounded out, grinning and licking and checking out the bag of takeaway in Andrew's hand. 'Get off, you rude dog,' he said affectionately, pushing her away, and ushered Libby in. 'Welcome to my home,' he said, and she knew he meant it, knew this and not the 'crumbling pile of dry rot' that he loved in spite of himself was where he came to recharge his batteries.

She looked around, at the heavily beamed walls and ceilings, the simple furnishings, the clean, unfussy lines.

It was him, through and through, and she could see him here so easily, so absolutely. 'I love it,' she said, unable to hold back her smile. 'Oh, I love it. It's beautiful. How did you find it?'

He laughed. 'Easy. It was falling down. I bought it five years ago, and I've been working on it ever since.'

'You have?' she said, surprised, and he shrugged.

'Not all of it, of course, but I've done a lot of the sandblasting of the beams and decorating and stuff like that, and I've done all the garden landscaping. It's how I relax. I'll show you round later, but we ought to eat this now or it'll be cold.'

He led her through to a huge open room, with a kitchen at one end, a dining area in the middle and comfortable, welcoming seating at the other end, where Will and Sally had made themselves at home.

'Grub's up,' Andrew said, waving the bag, and they got up and came over, kissing her on the cheek, greeting her like an old friend, and she felt a flicker of guilt that she'd deceived them at the weekend. Not now, though. Now, it seemed, they did have a relationship of sorts, although she wasn't quite sure what sort. Time would no doubt tell.

Andrew put the bag down in the middle of the table, ripped the tops off the containers, stuck spoons in them and they all helped themselves, piling their plates with the delicious, fragrant food. There were bottles of beer standing on the table, condensation running down the outsides, and even though it was cool outside she was beginning to think her cream jumper might be over the top. The house was gorgeously warm, and she could feel the glow coming off the wood-burner behind her.

'So, what time's your appointment tomorrow, Sally?' Andrew asked.

'Ten. And then I think I might go and do a little light shopping.'

Will groaned. 'Not more baby stuff. How much is that going to cost me?'

She laughed and patted his cheek. 'Less than you think. I might even get you a new pair of jeans. Those are dreadful.'

'They're nicely broken in. Leave me alone, you sound like my mother. If you want to do something useful, you can pass me a chunk of Peshwari naan.'

Andrew chuckled. 'You won't get him out of those jeans, Sally, unless you cut them up,' he advised softly, passing the basket of naan breads. 'He's welded to them.'

Her eyes sparkled. 'Now, there's a thought. Got any scissors, Andrew?'

'Forget it. They're my jeans,' Will said, looking as if he didn't quite trust her not to do it.

'They don't look any worse than the ones you were wearing on Saturday,' Libby told Andrew, and he grinned.

'Family trait. We like knackered old jeans.'

'Rebellion?'

'Nah. Antiques. You saw the rug in the hall.'

She laughed and helped herself to another scoop of butter chicken, resigned to eating lettuce the following day if necessary, and allowed herself to relax into the affectionate banter. It was lovely to see them off duty, to see the interaction between Andrew and Will, to see him as a brother as well as a doctor.

They talked about anything and everything, comfortable, relaxed, and after they'd finished eating they cleared the table and hid the leftovers from Lara, then migrated to the sofas that bracketed the wood-burner and Andrew put his arm round her and tucked her against his side. She wondered what Will would make of that, and the wisdom of it, of leaving herself wide open to hurt when she knew this was going nowhere.

But Andrew was just as wide open, and maybe he was beginning to rethink his stand on staying single.

Not that he'd be thinking of her in all that, of course not. They were poles apart. But lying there on the sofa with his arm around her, somehow they didn't seem so far apart, just a man and a woman, relaxing with family and being normal. He was probably just lonely, and enjoying her company. She'd do the same, take it at face value, enjoy it while it lasted and be grateful.

'Thank you for inviting me,' she said later, as they lay entangled in the huge bed that sat squarely opposite the curtainless window of his bedroom. 'I didn't like to muscle in, but they didn't seem to mind at all.'

He trailed a finger idly over her shoulder. 'They don't. They really like you.'

'I like them, too. Sally's gorgeous. She'll be a lovely mother. When's the baby due?'

'Six weeks, I think. She's having it in the Audley, so no doubt I'll get a call from Will all panic-stricken when she goes into labour.'

'Do you think he'll panic?'

'Will? Definitely. He doesn't care what he does to himself, but he's incredibly protective of Sally. It's just a pity he can't see that it cuts both ways.'

She snuggled closer. 'He is a bit of an idiot, isn't he? But he's fun.'

'Oh, yes. He's lots of fun. He's the face of the family now, really, the high-profile one. He loves all the publicity and drama—I just hate it. I'm happy to let him get on with it. I just wish I wasn't going to inherit it all at the end. He'd be much better at it—look at the way he handles all the charity stuff.'

She shifted so they were face to face and she could see his eyes. 'Does it worry you, living in his shadow?' she asked softly, and for a moment he said nothing, a thousand expressions flitting over his face in the moonlight, and finally he gave a low laugh.

'That's a strange remark.'

'Is it? It's how I see you both. He's like a tumbling, cascading waterfall, hurtling through life sparkling with sunlight and sweeping everyone along with him, whereas you're the smooth water, the still, quiet river, the surface unruffled but underneath teeming with life, sustaining it all without fuss.'

His brow creased. 'Is that a bad thing?'

'No! Absolutely not. It's just the way you both are. I

wondered if it was always like that, if he was always the brash, colourful one that everyone noticed. Chris said you used to be a bit of a wild child.'

He frowned slightly. 'That was a long time ago. And as for Will, they certainly noticed him when he went off the rails. I was constantly hauling his backside out of trouble—but I'm quite happy to let him overshadow me now. Frankly he's welcome to the limelight. I'm just surprised you picked up on it.'

'Why?'

He shrugged. 'It's just that most people don't see it like that,' he murmured, his voice quietly resigned. 'They think I'm the dull one, and Will's the interesting one—but I guess it's OK. I'm used to it now. And it suits me, really. Leaves me free to do what I want to do without an audience. My life hasn't really changed because of his illness, but his has. I'm still a doctor, still doing what I would have done before, although the emphasis might have changed slightly, but essentially I'm still doing what I set out to do in the first place.'

'And Will? He said he was only estate manager because he was too lazy to do anything else. Is that true?'

Andrew shook his head. 'No. He didn't do well at school after he was ill—his life was thrown into chaos, and when he recovered he lost the plot a bit and turned into a party animal. He's settled down a bit, of course, but he threw away his chance of going to uni, which was a shame, because he wanted to be an architect. I don't think he minds, though. As I said, he loves the estate and he's brilliant at running it.'

'Chris Turner said you would have given up medicine to come home and look after him if necessary.'

His smile was wry. 'Did he? Who knows? Luckily I

didn't have to, but the whole business might have changed my focus, though.'

'In what way?'

'I would always have gone into orthopaedics, but probably not paediatrics,' he admitted honestly. 'Especially after finding out I can't have kids. It's a bit like rubbing salt into the wound on a daily basis, but at least I get to spend time with children. It's bitter-sweet, really, and it can be stressful. Losing little patients is much harder than losing older ones. They've got so much ahead of them, so much to live for, and telling their parents they've lost their fight, or that their lives are going to be changed for ever—that's hard. I get down sometimes, doing that. If I'd known what I know now, I might not have done it, but I did, and I wouldn't change it now. I couldn't walk away from them, even if I spend every day being reminded that I'll never have any of my own.'

'You might. There are all sorts of things they can do with IVF these days.'

'I know, but not if there isn't anything there to work with.'

'You could find out.'

He shook his head. 'Libby, I know. There's no point beating myself up about it. I've accepted it. Just let it go.'

He met her eyes, lifted a hand and stroked away the tear that had dribbled down from the corner of her eye and puddled against her nose, and the tender gesture unravelled her.

She sniffed, and he pulled her back into his arms and kissed away the tears, then made love to her again, slowly, tenderly, until she thought her heart would burst with love for him, this gentle, dedicated man who had so much to offer and did it so quietly, without fuss or fanfare or arrogance.

She would love him for ever, she realised, even though

this relationship would inevitably have to end, because he didn't do relationships, wouldn't marry, held himself back from commitment because of a fear that later he alone might not be enough for the woman he married—that he could imagine he wouldn't be enough for anyone horrified her. He had so much to offer, so much to love—if only he would give her a chance.

And, in fact, it might not even be an issue. She needed to talk to her sister, to find out how she was getting on and take that first step towards finding out if she herself was affected by the genetic blight that had afflicted her family, because at the moment, with such massive unresolved issues in her own life, Libby wasn't in a position herself to make a commitment to Andrew anyway.

Not until she had answers of her own…

# CHAPTER SEVEN

THE week flew by, and she saw Andrew every day.

Sometimes it was just to snatch coffee, sometimes they managed lunch too, but he rang her on Tuesday evening, and he spent Wednesday night with her.

On Thursday, Joel was allowed out of bed to sit in a chair for the first time, and although his parents were anxious about it, his neck fracture was stable, the halo was holding his head steady and although he was a little shaky, he was pleased to be able to see things from the right angle again.

He was sad to see Lucas go, though, and so was Libby. She'd grown fond of the sullen, stroppy teenager, and she saw him off that morning with mixed feelings.

'Promise you'll pop up and see us when you come in to the fracture clinic,' she said, and he nodded.

'Yeah, I'll come,' he agreed, and then to her surprise, he leant over and hugged her awkwardly. 'You're OK, Sister, d'you know that, man? You're a nag and all that, but you're OK.'

She laughed a little unsteadily and let him go. 'You take care of yourself. We'll see you soon,' she said, and watched him swing down the corridor on his crutches, his skill with them hugely improved after all the zooming around the ward he'd been doing while he'd driven them mad for the last week or so.

She went back onto the ward and found Andrew there, checking on a little girl who'd been brought in for surgery the previous day on her Achilles tendons. They were too short to allow her to stand except on tiptoe, and Andrew had lengthened them with a Z-plasty to enable her to stand and walk properly at last.

But now she was sore and unhappy, and he was trying to examine her without success while the mother held her new baby in her arms and tried to soothe little Chloe and keep her older son out of mischief at the same time. So where was the nurse who should have been with Andrew?

It looked like a situation that was rapidly heading out of control, and as she went over to them he looked up and gave her a relieved smile.

She didn't wait for him to ask for help, just scooped up the little girl she'd already cuddled several times that morning, and sat down on the bed with her cradled firmly in her arms so Andrew could look at her feet, which were taped up now into a normal position following her surgery.

'Hello, sweetheart! Goodness me, you're looking pretty now! Did Mummy bring you in a new T-shirt?'

She sniffed and nodded, and Libby duly admired the duck on her tummy. 'That's such a pretty duck. What colour is it? Is it green?'

She giggled round her thumb. 'No.'

'Is it blue?'

Another giggle. 'No!'

'I know! It's red!'

The thumb came out. 'No, it's not! It's yellow!'

Libby blinked and laughed. 'So it is—silly me. Fancy me getting it wrong. I'll have to go back to school!'

Andrew was straightening up, his examination complete, and he gave her a thoughtful look before turning to the mother. 'OK. That's lovely. Her feet are looking much better.'

'They look normal now. I can't believe it. I really didn't think they'd ever look like that,' the mother said, her eyes filling.

He squeezed her shoulder gently. 'I told you they would. The position's everything I could have hoped for and, given a few days for it to settle, I'm sure you'll find she'll be able to start standing soon and before you know it, she'll be running around with her brother, won't you, Chloe?'

'Will she be able to walk like me?' the brother asked, and Andrew smiled.

'I'm sure she will, very soon.'

'I'll have to hide my toys.'

'Or you could share them,' their mother suggested gently, making him pull a mulish face.

'Hey, it's good to share. You can have twice as much fun with two of you,' Libby offered, and with a smile at the family they left them to consider the ramifications of a little girl soon to be mobile for the first time.

'Thanks for that,' Andrew murmured as they walked away. 'Sam had to bail on me—she had a vomiting child to clean up. I thought I'd be OK but then the baby kicked off and Chloe started to cry.'

'She's going to be great, though. You've done a good job,' she said, and he shot her a grin.

'It was easy. So straightforward for something that makes so much difference. Who would have thought that a little zig-zag cut in a tendon could make the difference between being crippled and being normal?'

'Who, indeed. Lucas has gone, by the way.'

'I know. I saw him earlier and wished him luck. I'll see him in Outpatients.'

'Mmm. Remind him to come in and see us. I think the boys'll miss him.'

'I think you will,' he teased, and she smiled.

'You know, I think you might be right?'

Andrew opened his mouth, but then his pager went off and he gave her a wry grin. 'That'll teach me to think about coffee,' he said with a groan. 'I'll see you later.'

He did, but only fleetingly. He came onto the ward to check Chloe and found Libby cuddling her again, because mum had gone home to feed and change the baby, taking her big brother, and wouldn't be back for a while. And even though Libby's shift was over, she couldn't leave the little one sobbing her heart out alone.

'I thought you'd finished?' he said softly, crouching down beside them and grinning at Chloe. 'Hi, sweets. Are you OK?'

'Want Mummy,' she said, and cuddled into Libby's chest, her heart-rending sobs tugging at him.

'I think her pain relief needs looking at,' Libby murmured, and he nodded and checked the chart, upping the dose to give her a little extra cover to help her settle for the evening. 'While you're at it, Joel's been a bit uncomfortable. I think he might have a pin-track infection in one of his halo screws. I've sent a swab off to the lab.'

'I'll check him and write him up for something if necessary. When did you do the swab?'

'Twelve?'

'So it won't be back till lunchtime tomorrow. I'll have a look now.'

He straightened up. 'I'm on duty tonight—I'm covering

for Patrick Corrigan, and it looks like it'll be busy, so I probably won't see you later.'

'OK,' she said, stifling the disappointment. 'I've got lots to do tonight anyway.'

'It's the weekend tomorrow,' he said softly. 'We could— oh, rats, I'd better go,' he sighed, glancing at his pager. 'Look, I'll call you later. We'll arrange something.'

He strode away, his long legs eating up the ward, and she saw him turn into the bay containing the older boys— checking on Joel, as he'd promised. She rocked Chloe, torn between getting her the extra dose of pain relief and settling her to sleep, and wondered what he'd suggest they did this weekend.

Nothing like the previous one, she was sure, but she felt a flutter of nervous anticipation. A quiet dinner in? Taking her out to a restaurant? A walk in the park?

Maybe nothing much at all. Maybe he'd just want to spend the time alone, and maybe the something he'd said they'd arrange would turn out to be a very small something indeed.

'You're being ridiculous,' she muttered, and Chloe stirred slightly, silencing her. She *was* being ridiculous. She wasn't supposed to be letting her heart get involved.

Too late, of course. It had been too late for that the moment he'd kissed her in the park, after they'd had lunch in the folly and walked through the woods just six days ago.

Certainly too late by the time he'd made love to her on Saturday night, and by Sunday evening any hope of remaining detached had been firmly blown out of the water.

But she still wondered what they'd be doing this weekend...

Andrew was desperate to get Libby to himself. They'd been so busy at work that he'd hardly seen her.

Well, that wasn't true. Considering they weren't supposed to be having a relationship, he was seeing a crazy amount of her, but it still wasn't enough, and he wanted her to himself. And he wanted to do nothing. Go nowhere, do nothing, just chill. He wondered if she'd be horribly disappointed if he suggested that, but it had been a busy couple of weeks and he just needed some down-time.

They'd do the garden, he decided. He didn't know if she liked gardening, but his needed attention whether she liked it or not, so if she didn't he'd just have to cut the grass and leave the rest for another time, he decided.

Always assuming Jacob was doing all right. They'd lightened the sedation that morning and he'd become restless, so they'd increased the pain relief and he'd settled. The fixators on his legs and pelvis were doing a good job and Andrew had no intention of interfering with them. The bones were well aligned and he was healing fast, so it was best left, and because he wasn't on call and little Jacob was still stable by the evening, his weekend was his own. They would split it between the two houses, because of Kitty, but tonight he wanted to be in his own home, with Libby.

He picked her up when he'd finished work at seven and took her back to his house, filling her in on the way about Jacob's progress, and she thought he was more relaxed than she'd ever seen him.

Relaxed and open and—happy.

Chris Turner would be impressed, she thought, remembering his comments a week ago at dinner.

Exactly a week, in fact, since the dinner party for his mother's birthday. Only a week. Heavens. It seemed much more. They seemed to have done so much in that time, gone so far, and yet they'd gone nowhere. They were still skirting around the question of their relationship, still taking every moment as it came, and to expect anything else would be greedy, she told herself as Andrew disappeared for a shower.

He came back a few minutes later in his favourite worn old jeans and a heavy cotton shirt, rolled up his sleeves and cooked for her, while she perched on a stool at the breakfast bar and watched him, his hands quick and precise, the surgeon at work. He sliced and shredded and chopped, threw everything into a wok and stir-fried it, poured in a jar of sauce and served it up on a bed of rice.

'Wow,' she said, savouring the first mouthful. 'This is gorgeous.'

'It's my speciality—fork food in bottled sauce. I only cook things that can be eaten with one hand because I'm usually eating while I check my email or write a report, and I have a very limited repertoire, so enjoy it while you can, because you'll very quickly get sick of it.'

She chuckled, but his words made her think. Was he intending her to be around for long enough to grow tired of his choice of menu? Or was it, indeed, a very short list?

Whatever, she'd savour every moment.

'Do you like gardening?' he asked suddenly, and she glanced up and saw a frown pleating his forehead.

'Yes—well, I think so, but I don't really know. It all depends on what you call gardening. I've only got a tiny garden, but I love pottering in it and I'd like to do more. Why?'

'Because I need to cut the grass tomorrow and the hedge could do with trimming and some of the borders need a tweak, but I don't want to bore you to death.'

'You won't bore me to death. It sounds fun.'

His frown disappeared. 'Good,' he said softly, and she realised he'd been troubled about it.

Why? Because he didn't know her, of course. They'd hurtled into this relationship by accident, really, without thought or planning, and she was pretty sure Andrew didn't do that. She was also pretty sure that the only reason they were still seeing each other was because it was easy. She hadn't expected anything, hadn't demanded anything, and so long as they both kept it light and just enjoyed each other's company, it was harmless.

In theory.

And for now, at least, she could keep it that way. Her appointment with the genetic counsellor hadn't come through yet, so she could stall the decision she had to make that could have a lasting and devastating impact on her future, and live solely for the present.

She put it out of her mind, ate the food he'd cooked for her, drank a couple of glasses of wine and went to bed with him, falling asleep in his arms. And on Saturday morning, because it had rained overnight and the grass was too wet to cut, they had a lie-in and then drove to Ashenden.

'We'll see if my parents are around, maybe have a coffee, then we could have lunch in the pub and go for a walk, if you like.'

Will and Sally were just unloading shopping out of the boot of their car when they pulled up, and they all went into the main family kitchen and found Jane and Tony in front of the Aga, drinking coffee with the dogs snoring at their feet.

'Have you got a pot on the go there, Ma?' Will asked, and she nodded and filled four mugs and slid them across the table, throwing Libby a welcoming smile.

'It's lovely to see you again, Libby. Did you enjoy last weekend?'

'Oh, I did. It was wonderful. Thank you so much for including me.'

'Oh, it's a pleasure,' she said, and Libby could almost hear the wedding bells ringing. Oh, Andrew, she thought, and stifled a sigh. They'd be so disappointed if they knew the truth.

She sat and listened to them talking, Will and his father discussing estate business, Andrew chipping in and offering his opinion, and then Will glanced at his watch and drained his mug. 'We ought to be getting on. Sally's decided to decorate the nursery and I've been given the job. Why don't you two drop by on your way home after your walk and have tea?'

'OK. We won't be with you long, though, I've got things to do in the garden this afternoon.'

'Me, too,' Jane added, getting to her feet. 'I've got a major programme of replanting going on in the rose garden this season, and there are some old ones to come out and lots of perennials that need lifting, and I still haven't drawn up a plan. Tony, I could do with a hand with that, if you've got time.'

She bent over and dropped a kiss on Andrew's cheek, then smiled at Libby. 'I'm sorry we've got to rush off. I hope we'll see you again soon—perhaps Andrew will bring you over for supper one night.'

'Of course I will,' Andrew said easily, getting to his feet as they left, and then he scooped up the mugs, put them in the dishwasher and turned to Libby. 'Shall we make a move?'

Lunch in the pub was lovely.

She started by looking at the pudding menu, chose the end of her meal and then planned the beginning, while Andrew rolled his eyes and chuckled.

'What? *What*? Why waste a good pudding by getting too full first?'

'Women. So what are you having?'

'Raspberry crème brûlée, preceded by crayfish and scallop risotto—or maybe I want the rice pudding, in which case the risotto is silly,' she said, making him laugh again.

'The risotto's gorgeous, and so's the crème brûlée. Have the rice pudding another time.'

'Or you could have it and we could share.'

He chuckled. 'We could. I was going to have apple crumble.'

'Oh! That's nice, too—stop laughing at me!'

She had the risotto in the end, and stole some of his pan-fried chicken liver and bacon salad, and they shared the puddings over coffee, which meant they were running out of time.

'Do you still want a walk, or tea with Will and Sally? We haven't really got time for both if I'm going to cut the grass.'

'Will and Sally?' she suggested, and he nodded.

'Good idea. We can see this nursery and admire their handiwork.'

She'd only been in the hall of the east wing, and she was looking forward to seeing the rest of it. She was busy thinking that the entrance was a bit of a disappointment, however, when it dawned on her that it was actually the back door.

There was a bell push, but Andrew just knocked and walked in, to find Sally in the kitchen in Will's arms. 'Put her down,' he said drily, and Will grunted, dropped a tender, lingering kiss on Sally's lips and let her go.

'Spoilsport. I'm just taking advantage of the last few weeks of having my wife to myself before it all comes to a grinding halt. How was lunch?'

'Lovely. I ate too much,' Libby confessed, and Sally laughed.

'Oh, you wait till you're pregnant. You can't eat a darned

thing without feeling full, and then ten seconds later you're starving again! I've turned into a herbivore—I graze constantly. Tea or coffee?'

'Coffee,' Andrew said, and Libby said nothing, because Sally's words were echoing in her head. If she stayed with Andrew, managed to convince him that they'd be happy together, she'd never be pregnant, never know what Sally was talking about, never have to decorate a nursery or walk the landing all night with a grizzly baby or go to a parents' evening and get roped into the PTA.

'We've just had coffee,' she said, coming to at last, but Will just grinned.

'Ah, but this is good coffee, not Ma's decaf rubbish or the stuff they serve in the pub. And we've got serious chocolate biscuits.'

She opened her mouth to say no, caught sight of the packet Will was waggling and buckled. 'Oh, well, then, that's different,' she said with a laugh, and after they'd admired Will's handiwork in the nursery, they ended up sitting around the table in the kitchen—a huge room with high ceilings and glorious views over the river—and drinking coffee and eating biscuits for over an hour before Andrew stood up and pulled her to her feet.

'Come on, or it'll be dark before we get home and get that grass cut,' he said, and something about the word 'home' just took her breath away.

No, she told herself, getting to her feet and saying goodbye to the others. It was just a figure of speech, a casual remark. It wasn't home—not hers, not *theirs*, no matter how ludicrously tempting it sounded. Home was her little house, with Kitty and her redundant duster and vacuum cleaner and the washing machine that thought it had been pensioned off, not Andrew's beautiful barn with its spectacular views and rustic charm.

And she'd better not forget it.


The next week was busy, as ever, and they fell into the pattern of the previous week. They met for coffee whenever they could, snatching a few minutes here and there, and if they could they'd have lunch, but more often they'd meet up after work and spend the night together in one house or the other. And for people who weren't supposed to be having a relationship, Libby thought, they were actually doing a fine job of it!

They went over for supper with Will and Sally on Tuesday night, and because he'd got away early and it was a beautiful evening, they went out into the park and walked around the Great Wood before supper, the dogs milling around their feet and sending a small herd of deer fleeing into the cover, vanishing like mist.

The sun was setting over the fields in the distance, the sky shot with red and gold, and as she strolled along with Andrew, she thought she'd never been so happy.

They went back to the house for supper, eaten in the kitchen, and because Sally was tired and they had to work in the morning, they left early and went back—to Andrew's house, yet again, for the night, and she lay in his arms and listened to the sound of his heart as she fell asleep.


'Are you going on holiday this year?' he asked casually the next morning as they were lying together contemplating the unwelcome thought of getting out of bed.

'Maybe, later on when my bank account's recovered from last year's extravagance. Why?'

'Make sure your passport's valid. I had to look at mine

yesterday because I've got a conference coming up and I'll need it, and I've had it so long I couldn't remember when it expires. It's just so easy to overlook and then you check just before you go and all hell breaks loose. It's happened to me before and it was a nightmare. I only just got it back in time.'

She ran a fingertip over his chin and down his throat, relishing the rough rasp of his morning beard. 'So you aren't about to whisk me away anywhere exotic, then?' she teased, hoping he'd say yes, but he just chuckled.

'Sadly not, but it's an idea. I suppose you could come to this conference with me, if you aren't doing anything else, but it might be rather dull, though. They tend to be a bit hectic and it's only in Brussels, not very exotic at all.'

'Oh, you make it sound so exciting,' she said drily. 'I think I'll pass.'

'They don't run all night,' he murmured, and she snuggled back down with her head on his chest, listening to the steady, even beat of his heart under her ear.

'No, I suppose they don't. You'd have to make it irresistible, though, to tempt me.'

His laugh rumbled under her ear. 'Well, you'd better check your passport when you get home, hadn't you? It would be a shame if you talk me into taking you and then you end up not being able to come after all.'

She felt a little twinge of disappointment that it was only an afterthought and he didn't sound over-enthusiastic, but that was silly. Why on earth should he be thinking of taking her away? Not that they needed to go away, anyway, because just to be here with him was all that she asked.

She loved waking up in his house, with the uncurtained window overlooking open countryside just there at the foot of the bed, so they could lie there and stare out across the fields and not see a soul. And despite all her attempts to hold herself in check, it was beginning to feel more and more like home, and staying there was getting to be a habit.

'It's so lovely here,' she murmured. 'Really peaceful.'

'It is. I love it. I could stay here all day.'

'Sadly not,' she said drily, and sighed. 'Poor Kitty. I'm beginning to feel so guilty about her. She must think I don't love her any more.'

'We'll stay there tonight,' he said. 'And all weekend. Will and Sally are tied up with a charity event on Sunday at Ashenden, and I'm keeping well out of it. We can get pizza and a DVD and lie in front of the telly with the cat and feed her cheese.'

'You do realise she's just a cupboard lover, don't you?' Libby said drily, prising herself off his chest and getting out of bed. 'I'm going to shower or I'll be late for work.'

'I need to get in early, too. I'll shower with you.'

'So, tell me, how is this going to speed things up?' she asked, as he took her into his arms under the pounding spray and kissed her thoroughly.

'Multi-tasking,' he said, and muffled her laughter with his kiss.

She'd wondered, as he'd made love to her in the shower, how long it would be before the bubble burst, and later that morning something happened that brought reality home with a vengeance.

Andrew appeared on the ward holding a set of notes, and paused at the nurses' station. 'Could we have a word?' he murmured, and she smiled.

'Could we have a word,' was code for 'come into the office, I want to hug you,' but once they were in there, his first words drove all such thoughts out of her head.

'I've got a patient coming in later today that I wanted

to talk to you about. Briefly, he had a fall from his wheel-chair two weeks ago and broke his arm, but he's getting pins and needles now. I reviewed it yesterday in the fracture clinic and it needs surgery, so I'm admitting him. The problem is he's got DMD.'

DMD. Duchenne muscular dystrophy. She felt the blood drain out of her face, and she had to remind herself to breathe.

'His heart isn't great and his $pCO_2$ is high—his lungs are very compromised because of pronounced scoliosis, so he's not a good surgical risk, but the cardiologist and physicians are going to review him tomorrow and we'll see if we think we can go ahead with the arm under general anaesthetic. Otherwise I'll have to do it with a nerve block and mild sedation, but that's a bit grim for a kid, and for his parents.'

She nodded, still reeling. Why? Why now, of all the times, when she'd just discovered how much it mattered that she wasn't—?

'OK, this is the picture show,' he said, snapping plates up onto the box light in the office. 'Here's the arm—you can see how it's displaced now, compared to straight after the fracture. And this is his spine. You can see the curvature here—and this was two years ago. It's worse now. His lung capacity is becoming more compromised, and he's finding it all more uncomfortable, but we can't do that kind of op here and at the moment I'm just concerned with his arm. His spine needs review at a specialist centre, and I intend to refer him as soon as this arm is sorted to see if they can do something to improve the quality of his life. I just hope he's up to it but I'm afraid it might have been left too late.'

Libby studied the plates with a frown. She wasn't an expert on DMD by any means, but she'd been reading up on it recently, and she forced herself to recall the facts—not hard, under the circumstances, but hard to think clearly.

It was a progressive, inherited degenerative muscle disorder that affected boys almost exclusively, and girls carrying the defective gene were usually although not always unaffected. The deterioration, caused by a lack of dystrophin in the muscles, slowly but surely crippled the person until their body was unable to support itself. They usually died of heart or lung problems in their teens or twenties due to severe scoliosis compressing the chest cavity, but the spinal curvature was one of the things that could be improved. However, even she could see it didn't look good and the surgeons were going to have their work cut out to fix it—assuming the young lad got the chance. 'How old is...' she peered at the plates '...Craig?'

'Sixteen—so technically he's on the cusp of moving up to the adult ward, but as it's me who's dealing with him I wanted him on Paeds—it's more fun, and he's short on fun at the moment. Nice lad. You'll like him. Good sense of humour.'

She tried to smile. She'd met more than enough brave kids who made light of their situation with humour, and the worse it was, the funnier they could be. Till you caught them unawares and saw their true feelings. It wasn't so funny then. 'How long's he got?' she asked quietly, holding her breath for his answer.

Andrew shrugged. 'Who knows? His heart's enlarged, his body's very weak now—the muscles are packing up faster than I'd have expected. He's been in a wheelchair for five years already, so he's not going to make old bones, but he's still in full-time education, he's as bright as a button and he's amazingly gutsy. I just hope they can give him a while longer and make him more comfortable, but that all depends on the cardiac and pulmonary assessments—and first we have to sort this arm.'

She nodded slowly. 'OK. I'll arrange a bed for him. Do you want him in with the boys, or on his own?

'Oh, in with the boys. Joel's bored to death. They can entertain each other for the next few days. Right, I have to go, but I'll be back later with the MDT—can I leave this with you?'

'Yes, sure,' she said, her eyes fixed on the X-ray plates, and he kissed her cheek and went out, leaving her standing there staring at the havoc wrought by this slow and insidious killer gene. A gene that was killing her cousin inch by inch.

A gene which, if she had inherited it from her mother's side of the family, would make her a carrier...

# CHAPTER EIGHT

CRAIG was admitted an hour later, and she'd put him opposite Joel so they could see each other.

It was no good putting them side by side, since Joel couldn't turn his head with the halo splint, and as Craig was most likely to need nursing propped up in bed, it was the best way for them to be placed.

Luckily the boys' bay was quiet now. Christopher and Jonathan, the twins who'd fallen out of the tree and broken their legs, had gone home before the weekend, and the other beds had post-op fractures and ligament repairs, comparatively minor injuries which had needed surgery but didn't necessitate a long stay, so she was happy to shuffle them to make way for the boys who might well have longer to go.

Andrew was right—Craig was struggling. Every breath was a physical effort, every word took energy he didn't have, but his eyes were bright and alert and he was open and friendly. 'I've put you here,' she told him. 'This is Joel. I'll let him tell you why he's in here and what he's done to himself. Mr Langham-Jones said you'd got a good sense of humour!'

Craig chuckled and raised his hand to Joel. 'Hi, there. I'm Craig.'

'What happened to you?'

'I fell out of my wheelchair. It didn't like the kerb. What about you?'

'I fell through the roof of the conservatory.'

'What, glass?' Craig asked, looking suitably impressed.

'No. The wooden panel by the house. It's meant to be a fire escape, but it was rotten and I fell through it. Well, one leg did. The other one didn't, so I swivelled round and went off the edge head first and broke my neck. I was supposed to be going home but I've got an infection where the screws go into my skull.'

'Oh, gross!' Craig said, pulling a face. Libby chuckled and handed him the tubes so he could insert the soft prongs into his nose and link himself up to the oxygen. He did it without even looking at them, an indication of how much he'd had to do with hospitals and oxygen over the past few years, and she had to fight the twin urges to hug him and run away.

She did neither, the soft voice behind her murmuring her name jerking her out of her turbulent thoughts.

'Andrew!' She looked up, distracted, her head miles away on the other side of the country at a funeral, meeting her seventeen-year-old cousin, Edward, for the first—and probably last—time.

His brow pleated into a frown. 'Are you OK?' he murmured softly, and she nodded.

She wasn't. She was far from OK, she'd been slapped in the face by reality, forced to confront what her future might have been had she been born a boy. What the future might be for any potential son she bore.

'I'm fine,' she lied. 'I'll get the paperwork. When's the MDT meeting?'

'As soon as I tell them he's here,' he said quietly. 'We've gone through the notes, they want to meet him. I was just popping up to say hi and put him in the picture. Could you page them?'

'Sure, I'll go and do it now,' she said, and leaving the boy in Andrew's capable hands, she retreated to the relative sanctuary of her office.

He followed her in there a few moments later, shutting the door and giving her an odd look. 'Libby, is everything all right?'

'It's fine.'

'No, it's not. It's not fine. There's something the matter.'

'Andrew, I'm fine,' she insisted. 'I'm just busy.'

Busy, and unable to find the words to tell him, to bring the truth out into the open and give voice to it, because by doing so she'd be facing up to it and admitting that there was a possibility that she was a carrier of DMD.


'Good news. We can do Craig's arm under GA tomorrow,' he told her over the phone that night.

'That's great,' she said, trying to sound cheerful. 'So what's the bad news?'

'I'm tied up here and I won't get to you. I've had another look at Craig's X-rays and I want to go over the notes again, do a bit more research, and I'll be really late, so I might as well kip here. I'll see you here tomorrow.'

'I take it you're still at work, then?'

He gave a rusty chuckle. 'Yes, I'm still at work. I'm sorry. I thought—'

'What?'

He hesitated, then sighed. 'Nothing. I'll see you in the morning. Sleep well.'

'You, too. Try not to be up all night.'

'I won't. Take care.'

She stared at the phone. Damn. She'd geared herself up

to talk to him, decided to tell him when he got to her house. And now he wasn't coming.

There was no way she could do it at work, so she'd have to tell him tomorrow night. Another twenty-four hours.

She went to bed, too troubled to sleep at first, but she was woken later by her phone. She struggled up on one elbow and picked it up, scraping the hair back out of her eyes with the other hand and peering at the clock. Two-thirty? 'Hello?' she murmured.

'It's me. I'm outside—can you let me in?'

Andrew. She slipped out of bed, ran down and opened the door, and he stepped inside and pulled her into his arms for a hug.

'I thought you weren't coming?' she mumbled into his shirtfront, and he eased her away and looked down into her sleep-glazed eyes.

'I wasn't, but—I don't know, there was something in your voice, and you keep telling me you're all right, but I know you're not. I know there's something wrong, and I just couldn't settle until I knew what it was.'

She turned her head away, but not before he saw the slight sheen of tears. 'You're right. I need to talk to you. There's something you don't know—something even I don't know yet.'

His heart pounded. He had no idea what it was, but his imagination was running riot and it wasn't coming up with anything good. 'OK. Let's go somewhere comfortable and talk about it.'

'Bed?' she suggested, and he nodded and shrugged off his jacket, hanging it over the end of the banisters as they went up the stairs to her room.

And as soon as they were settled in bed, with his arms around her cradling her against his shoulder, she carried on, 'I went to a funeral just over a year ago, of a great-great-aunt. And I met a young man there—a cousin. He was in a wheelchair.' She swallowed. 'He looked a lot like Craig.'

He felt a cold chill run over him. 'DMD?' he said, tilting her chin so he could see into her eyes.

She nodded, and he shook his head slowly. No wonder she'd been looking a little strange today, as if things weren't quite right with her world. Of all the cruel twists of fate, to have Craig on the ward. 'You didn't know about it?'

She shook her head. 'No. I had no idea. It's an X-linked recessive, so it doesn't show up in girls, and I've only got one sister, and my mother's an only child, and her mother was one of two girls. There's no evidence of it on our side of the family.'

'And this cousin?'

'He's on the other side, my great-aunt's side. We had no idea. We don't have any contact with them, really, because we're spread out all over the place. It was a complete bolt from the blue.'

'I'm sure. Oh, Libby, I'm so sorry,' he murmured, aching for her, this woman who was so good with children, a woman just made to be a mother, and the implications this could have for her. 'And you?' he asked, holding his breath for the answer. 'Are you a carrier?'

She shrugged, her face unhappy. 'I don't know. My sister Jenny and her husband were trying for another baby at the time, and they stopped immediately and went for genetic screening to find out, and discovered that she's a carrier. Luckily their first child's a girl, so they're having her screened, but they won't have any more.'

'Why? They can, with IVF.'

'I know, but apparently they just screen for sex rather than the gene, and implant female embryos, so you can still hand the gene on even if the carrier's unaffected, and Jenny says she couldn't do that. It's just handing the dilemma on to the next generation and, anyway, IVF's not exactly plain sailing, there's no guarantee it will work and there's still a chance of having a child with a disability because of the possibility of a damaged embryo. The embryo screening process isn't without risk, and it strikes me it's just swapping a known risk for an unknown one, and I'm not sure I'll want to do that, either.'

'You're getting ahead of yourself,' he pointed out gently. 'You don't even know yet if you *are* a carrier, do you? Are you waiting for results?'

She shook her head. 'No. I saw my GP about getting screened, but because I wasn't in a relationship and not seeking to become pregnant any time in the foreseeable future, there didn't seem to be any hurry.'

He let his breath out on a long, quiet sigh and drew her closer into his arms, deeply saddened for her. 'I'm so sorry. I had no idea you were going through all that.'

'Of course you didn't. Why should you? And I haven't really been going through it, I've been avoiding it, because it wasn't relevant and frankly I'd rather not know. Except now, seeing Craig today—well, I have to know, don't I? I have to find out. I can't just ignore it any longer. I can't afford to take the risk of bringing a child into the world to suffer like that. And he's so brave and so candid...'

Her voice broke, and he cradled her against his chest while she cried, not only for Craig, but for the uncertainty in her future, for the very real possibility that having children, at least naturally conceived children, might be denied her. It was something everyone took for granted, and he knew only too well how hard it was to come to terms with when it was taken away.

\* \* \*

'Are you all right?'

Craig nodded sleepily, the pre-med taking effect. 'Yeah, I'm fine. Can't breathe very well, but that's par.'

She helped him shift, propped another pillow under his head and adjusted the flow of his oxygen. 'Better?'

'Yeah. Thanks.'

'My pleasure. The arm's a bit of a pain really, isn't it?' she added softly, and he gave her a tired smile.

'Yes. I could have done without it, but if I get through the GA, at least it'll prove I'm a good anaesthetic risk.'

She tipped her head on one side at his choice of words. 'Good working knowledge, too much practical experience or doctor in the family?' she asked, and he chuckled.

'All the above. I thought I'd want to train as a doctor if I stayed alive that long, but it's unlikely so I've adjusted my expectations. If they can straighten my scoliosis, or at least stop it getting worse, there's more chance, but I still think it's a long shot. Pity, really. I'd be good—lots of empathy!'

She laughed with him, touched by his straightforward acceptance of his condition, by the courage he showed in the face of an operation which, while routine in anyone else, could possibly cost him his life.

No. That was stretching it too far. Andrew wouldn't operate under GA if the team didn't feel it was feasible.

This time.

So what about next?

A shiver ran over her, and she was glad when the porter came to take him to Theatre. She walked up with him, not because his case meant more to her than any of the others but because of his courage, because despite it, she knew he had to be a little bit afraid.

'I'll see you later,' she said as the anaesthetist started the

drugs, and he winked at her, his eyes glazing as the anaesthetic took effect.

'OK?'

Andrew was standing waiting, and she saw his eyes
concerned above the mask.

'Fine. He's OK with it.'

His eyes studied hers for a second. They both knew he
wasn't asking about Craig, but about her, and she smiled
and nodded assurance.

His eyes creased in a smile. 'Good. We'll see you in a
bit. It shouldn't take long. I'll let you know.'

Craig was due back on the ward later that afternoon, after
a lengthy period in Recovery, but he'd done well, according to Andrew, it had all gone according to plan, he'd coped
well with the anaesthetic and he would be fine. Nevertheless, she'd be glad to see him back in his bed.

So would his mother, who'd made herself scarce when
he was going up to Theatre so she didn't embarrass him,
but ever since had sat in silent vigil by his wheelchair,
waiting for his return.

'He'll be back soon,' Libby told her. She'd made them
both a cup of tea at the end of her shift, and they were
sitting drinking it while they waited.

'It's funny. I've known for years we were going to lose
him, but this fracture has been a bit of an eye-opener. I
mean, you expect him to die of cardiac problems or pneu-
monia, not a broken arm. And he could have done. If it had
gone wrong—'

'But it didn't, and they wouldn't have operated like that
if they'd felt it would. They would have done it with a local
anaesthetic, but it wouldn't have been very nice for him.'

His mother laughed a little bitterly. 'None of it's very

nice for him. We were really shocked when we learned what he'd got. There isn't any of it in the family anywhere that we can trace. It's just one of those things.'

'It happens like that sometimes,' she said. 'A freaky gene—a bit of damage. Things go wrong spontaneously from time to time.'

'I know. But why did it have to be my boy?' she asked, and Libby could see her eyes were filled with a sadness that ran too deep for tears.

'Change of plan,' Andrew told her on Thursday evening when he arrived at her house armed with the makings of supper.

'Change of what plan?'

'The weekend,' he said, buzzing her cheek with a kiss and grinning cheerfully. 'We're going to London tomorrow night and we won't be back till Sunday. Pack smart casual and something a bit dressier for going out for dinner—and bring a warm coat for walking by the river, and comfortable shoes for sightseeing.'

'Sightseeing?' she said, bemused, and he smiled.

'Don't tell me you've seen everything?' he asked. 'And even if you have, you haven't seen it with me, so just do as you're asked and go and pack while I get the supper.'

She felt a little fizzle of excitement, just at the thought of going away with him, but—London? It was so dreary in the winter, but of course with him it would be different. More fun. Everything was more fun with him. 'I'll have to get Amy or someone to feed the cat. I hope she can.'

'So do I. I'm tired. I want to get away.' He hesitated, frowning. 'Unless you really don't want to?'

'No, I'd love to, of course I would,' she said hastily, because he was tired, and he did need to get away. Away from his family, from the hospital, from all of it. And so did she. She desperately needed some downtime with him, and the idea of going away with him was suddenly wonderfully appealing.

'It sounds lovely,' she said with another smile, and ran upstairs to pack, thanking her lucky stars that she'd done the washing the night before and it was dry. She packed her best matching underwear, a nightdress and light dressing gown for the hotel, trousers, her little black dress, flat shoes, heels, pretty tops, and left out her decent black trousers and a pretty jumper for travelling down the next night.

'Done,' she said as she went back into the kitchen, and he smiled and held out his arms.

'Good girl. Now come and give me a hug, and then you can help me make the supper.'

'Make it?' she said, leaning back and laughing up at him. 'It's pizza and salad!'

'I told you not to expect too much of my culinary skills,' he grinned, releasing her and swatting her on the bottom. 'Come on, open the bag of salad and let's eat. I'm starving and the pizza's done.'

# CHAPTER NINE

SHE rushed home after work on Friday, changed quickly into her decent black trousers, her favourite boots which were comfortable enough for sightseeing and decent enough for dinner when they arrived in London, and was ready and waiting when he pulled up at her door.

He came in, kissed her and then hesitated. 'Um—I lied to you,' he said softly, his eyes sparkling and an air of suppressed excitement about him. 'I hope you weren't fudging when you said you had a valid passport?'

She stared at him, her jaw dropping, and laughed in surprise. 'Passport?'

'Come on, we need to get a move-on. It is here, I take it?'

The look of panic on his face was comical, and she laughed again and opened the dresser drawer, waggling it under his nose. 'Here—all present and correct, valid for four and a half years. How long a trip were you planning?'

He laughed. 'Sadly only two nights. Come on.'

'Where are we going?' she asked, but he just tapped the side of his nose, helped her into her coat, pocketed her passport and put her case in the car while she locked the house.

'Andrew, where are we going?' she asked, butterflies

having a field day in her stomach now, and he slid behind the wheel, shot her a grin and said,

'Paris.'

She felt her jaw drop. 'Paris?' she squeaked.

He shrugged. 'Well, when I asked you two weeks ago what you'd be doing over the weekend, that was what you said, and it sounded like a fantasy. So I thought I'd make it come true for you. Except we're not flying, we're going on the Eurostar from St Pancras.'

'That's fine,' she said a little weakly. 'I hate flying.'

They arrived at their hotel shortly before midnight, and when they went into the room, all she could see through the huge windows was the twinkle of a million lights. 'Oh, Andrew!' she breathed, crossing to the glass and staring out in awe.

They could see the bridges spanning the Seine, the arches illuminated in a rainbow of colours, and to their left the glittering Eiffel Tower soared skywards, with its flashing beam like a lighthouse sweeping across the night sky.

He slid his arms round her and eased her back against his chest. 'Enough lights for you?'

'Oh, yes!' She turned in his arms, lifting her face to his, and he lowered his head and touched his lips to hers.

'Good. Do you want anything from room service?'

'What, after that gorgeous meal on the train? I shouldn't think so.'

'Nothing to drink?'

'No. I'm happy drinking in the view. It's beautiful. Thank you so much for bringing me here.'

'My pleasure. It's lovely to get away.' He dropped a kiss on her nose and smiled down at her. 'Time for bed? We've got a long day tomorrow.'

She smiled. 'Bed sounds lovely,' she said softly, and going up on tiptoe, she kissed him back.

He hadn't lied about the long day, he thought as they strolled along the Seine.

Breakfast in a patisserie, followed by sightseeing in the morning, a lunchtime river cruise from the quayside near the foot of the Eiffel Tower, returning them two hours later, then a good stretch to the Musée d'Orsay further along the Rive Gauche, where Libby gazed up, fascinated, at the curved glass roof of the old station building that now housed a fabulous collection of artworks by the Impressionists—sculptures and paintings that Libby showed a surprising knowledge of.

'I did art history at A level,' she told him, studying a picture by Manet before strolling on to the next one. And the next. And the next.

She had stamina, he thought with an inward smile as they left the exhibition. They'd walked miles already, and now they walked again, taking the metro to Montmartre and strolling round hand in hand, steeping themselves in more art and architecture and history before heading back to the hotel.

They showered and changed, him into his suit, Libby into her little black dress that did shocking things to his blood pressure, then headed out again.

'Where are we going?' she asked yet again, but he just smiled and kept her guessing.

'The Eiffel Tower?' she asked hopefully as they approached it. 'I was guessing wildly, you know—can you even go up it at night?'

'I don't know,' he lied, the fast-pass tickets burning a hole in his pocket, but as they arrived at the bottom and skipped the queue she laughed crossly and told him off for teasing, and he could see she was excited. They went to the top in the lift, changing at the second floor and soaring right up to level three for the most spectacular view, and then came down, stopping at level two to change lifts again—except instead of changing lifts, he led her to the restaurant.

'We're eating here?' she said, awed, as they were shown to a seat by the window. 'How on earth did you get a reservation?'

He chuckled. 'Sleight of hand and very fortuitous luck. They had a group cancellation, apparently. Normally you have to book weeks in advance, even in the off season.'

She tipped her head on one side and searched his eyes. 'Andrew, how long have you been planning this?' she asked, and he smiled.

'Two weeks?'

'Two weeks? But—that was your mother's birthday weekend. We weren't even—well—whatever we're doing.'

She floundered to a halt, her eyes troubled, and he reached out and took her hand. 'Seeing each other?' he suggested softly. 'Going out?'

'We weren't supposed to be,' she reminded him, looking confused and a little wary, and he smiled again, confused and a little wary himself, but it was too late for that, and if things had been different—but they weren't, he thought with an inward sigh.

'I know,' he murmured. 'But it sounded as if it was your dream weekend, and so I made some enquiries.'

'And craftily checked that I had a passport.'

He laughed. 'Only after I'd booked it. I had a moment of panic that yours might have expired like mine had the time I told you about, or that it wouldn't be at your house.'

'Where else?' she said, frowning in puzzlement.

'I don't know—your parents'?'

She shook her head. 'My father's dead, and my mother lives in Cork, in Ireland, with her new husband. And apart from that, there's only my sister Jenny and her husband and daughter in Cumbria.'

He realised he hadn't known any of that. Well, apart from the fact that she had a sister. Other than her recent revelation about the DMD, she'd shared very little of herself. Part of their unspoken agreement to keep things between them light—except he wasn't doing too well on that front.

Take this weekend, for instance. He'd squandered a fortune on it without a second thought, just to spoil her because he—

He stopped dead, his thoughts slamming into a brick wall. He what?

He *loved her*?

No.

*Yes.*

The waiter appeared to take their order, and he put the disturbing thought on the back burner. For now.

It wouldn't stay there, though. As they strolled back to the hotel after their meal—only two delicious courses because even Libby, with her taste for desserts, had been defeated after the generous lunch on the river—he threaded his fingers through hers and drew her to a halt, turning to stare out over the river. It was cool, and he slid his arm round her, holding her close against his side as the wind whipped across the water and swirled around them.

'Happy?' he asked her, and she nodded, her face alight.

'Very. That was a fabulous meal, thank you so much,' she said, snuggling into his side. 'I hate to think what this is costing you.'

'It's irrelevant. It's just lovely to get right away, and I haven't had so much fun for years. It's been wonderful,' he admitted, 'and it's all because you're here with me.'

She turned in his arms, lifting her face to his, her eyes luminous in the lamplight. 'Oh, Andrew...'

He cradled her cheek in his hand, stroking the pad of his thumb against the delicate skin. 'I think I'm falling in love with you, Libby,' he confessed softly, and her mouth opened on a soundless O.

She closed it and smiled, reaching up to touch his face, her hand cool against his jaw. 'I *know* I'm falling in love with you,' she replied, her voice quiet, sincere.

He swallowed hard, staring into her guileless eyes, suddenly swamped by sadness.

'Oh, Libby,' he murmured, tracing her lovely face with his fingertips. 'This wasn't meant to happen. It was all supposed to be strictly no strings—that was what I promised you, and now...'

'Now we're having a wonderful time together. That's all. And anyway,' she said, the shadow returning to her eyes, 'it may not be the problem you imagine.'

'How can it not be?' he asked sadly. 'I wish—you'll never know how much—that things could be different, but they aren't. I can't give you children, Libby, and I can't ask you to sacrifice your chances of being a mother for me.'

'I'm not asking you to. We've talked about this. You know how I feel about having children if I'm a carrier.'

'But we don't know if you are.'

'I know, but if I *am* a carrier, then I won't have children, not with all the risks, so the fact that you can't have them might not be an issue,' she said, tilting her head back again so she could meet his eyes. 'We'd both be in the same position, so we could let our relationship take its course.'

He frowned down at her, stunned at the implications of her words. 'But you wouldn't be in the same position as me,' he argued. 'You could still have children, Libby. IVF's not that risky.'

'I know, but it isn't risk free, and if I was with someone who desperately wanted children and could otherwise have had them, I might go for it for their sake—but I'm not. I'm with someone who can't have them, and so I wouldn't have to make that painful choice and potentially live with the consequences of it every day of my child's life.'

He felt hope swell in his chest, and crushed it ruthlessly. He wouldn't let himself think about it, wish a carrier status on her so that he didn't have to lose her. And he still wasn't convinced that, years down the line, she wouldn't regret her decision if she chose to be with him and pass up on the chance to be a mother.

'Get the test results and then we'll talk about it again,' he said, stopping his mind from getting carried away with planning the future—a future with Libby in it.

He let her go, slipping his hand down her arm and taking her chilly hand. It was too cold to stand and talk, and anyway he wanted to take her to bed and hold her, to tell her without words how he felt for her.

'Come on, you're freezing,' he said gently. 'Let's go back to the hotel.'

He was sleeping, sprawled on his front across the bed, one bare, hair-strewn leg sticking out of the duvet, his head turned towards her.

He loved her—or so he said, but she wasn't sure.

Libby sat on the chair by the window watching him sleep, happy to let him rest so she could think through his reaction to their conversation.

He hadn't seemed convinced about her electing not to have children if she was a carrier, or her suggestion that if she was they could let their relationship take its course. Rather, he'd seemed almost—wary. He'd brought her back to the hotel and made love to her with aching tenderness, but she'd felt there was a part of himself he was holding back. A part he always held back.

Habit? Because, of course, he'd spent years denying himself a meaningful, long-term relationship on the grounds that he wouldn't let it go anywhere—or so he said. But what if that was just an excuse? What if he just didn't want to get married, and used it as a justifiable reason to avoid a permanent entanglement?

She had no idea. They hardly knew each other, even though they'd worked in the same unit for months. And they'd been together now for just two weeks. Two ecstatic, delirious, blissful weeks.

Weeks in which she'd fallen in love with him, and he, apparently, with her. Or had he? Had he really?

Restless, she got to her feet and padded softly over to the dresser unit to search for a magazine. Not that she could read it if it was in French. She was far from fluent, her schoolgirl French all but forgotten, but she could look at the pictures.

She drew a blank on the magazine front, but found a selection of tourist information leaflets, and flicked through them. Some were in several languages, including English, and she studied them while she waited for him to wake up.

Notre Dame, she thought. That looked interesting. Or perhaps the Louvre—

'Planning the day?'

She looked up, startled, and smiled at him. 'I didn't realise you were awake. I was just killing time.'

'You should have woken me.' He threw back the bed-clothes and walked over to her, bending to brush his lips against her cheek. 'I need the bathroom. You could call room service and get breakfast sent up, and we can plan our day over a jug of coffee and a pile of hot, buttery croissants.'

'Consider it done,' she said with a smile, and put her doubts out of her mind.

They got back to Audley at eleven that night, exhausted, and went straight to her house to feed the cat.

'Oh, Kitty, did you miss me?' she asked, scooping her up, but Kitty's only interest was food, as usual, and Libby just rolled her eyes, put her down and fed her. 'Do you want a drink?' she asked Andrew, but he shook his head.

'No, I need to get home,' he said, disappointing her. 'I've got things to do before tomorrow, and I ought to check my messages and give Will a ring before I go to bed, and I've got a long day. We're on duty overnight tomorrow and it could be a bit hectic, and if I stay—well, you know what'll happen,' he said ruefully, hugging her. 'But I'll see you in the morning. We'll have coffee, or lunch, or something, anyway.'

She nodded, hugging him back. 'Thank you so much for this weekend,' she said, loath to let it end, knowing he was right and that he had to get some sleep before the busy week ahead. So did she, but somehow when she was in his arms that didn't seem to matter. 'Go on, go home while I'll still let you,' she told him, and, kissing him lightly on the lips, she eased out of his arms and opened the door. 'I'll see you tomorrow.'

He kissed her again, then slid behind the wheel and drove away. She watched his lights disappear, then closed the door and went to find the cat and check her phone for messages.

And discovered that Jenny had phoned, leaving a message for her to call her back. She put her mobile on charge, because of course she'd forgotten to take her charger with her and it had gone flat, and when she checked it she found two missed calls and a text, all from her sister.

*RING ME!*

Dreading the call, desperately hoping it was the news her sister had been praying for, she rang.

He hadn't wanted to leave.

It was true, he did have things to do, and he needed to get some uninterrupted sleep, but when he eventually got into it, he found the bed cold and empty and just plain wrong without her.

He was an idiot. He should have seen the way it was going, realised what was happening to him—to them—and called a halt, instead of letting himself drift along getting sucked in deeper and deeper with a woman who frankly deserved better than a life of barren frustration with a man who could never give her children—the children she would be so wonderful with.

His chest ached, and he rubbed it with the heel of his hand. Heart ache? Was it possible for a heart really to ache?

Stress, he told himself. Too much coffee, too little sleep, too much rich food—nothing to do with the yawning void beside him where Libby ought to be.

He turned over, thumped the pillow and shut his eyes. He needed to sleep. He had children tomorrow who needed his full attention, awake and alert and on the ball, not running on empty. So he rolled onto his back again, and

tensed and relaxed all the muscle groups in his body in turn,
a trick he'd learned years ago, and eventually his body shut
down his mind and he slept.

'I had a message from my sister.'

Andrew stopped, his hand in mid-air, the coffee sus-
pended as Libby stood smiling at him in his office doorway.

'And?'

Her eyes misted over. 'Her daughter's OK. She's not
a carrier.'

Oh, hell, she was going to cry. He put the coffee down
and hugged her. 'That's great news. I'm really pleased for
her,' he said. He let her go, kissed her briefly and went back
to the coffee machine to pour another cup. 'So what now?'

'Now? I'm going to contact my GP again, chase up this
genetic screening referral. I have no idea how long it'll take.'

'Go private,' he said, shocking himself. 'I'll pay for it.
I know the consultant here—Huw Parry. He'll sort it for
you. I'll give him a ring.'

'I can't let you do that! Anyway, what are you going
to tell him?'

'Nothing. Just that a friend of mine needs to see him
urgently.'

'But it's not urgent!'

It felt urgent. It felt urgent to him, to know beyond
doubt that she wasn't a carrier, to know if he was holding
her in a relationship for his own selfish ends—a relationship she'd do better to move on from. And once he knew
that, he could set her free, cut himself off from her and end
their bitter-sweet affair.

'I think it's time you knew,' he said gently. Time they
both knew, to put an end to this selfish and sickening hope

that had arisen in him—and which disgusted him. Time to put a stop to it all before it destroyed him.

Libby stared at him, trying to read his eyes, and what she saw there didn't reassure her. Was he trying to find an excuse to get her out of his life? In which case, all he had to do was say so. Or was he seriously thinking about what she'd said, that if she was a carrier, she wouldn't have children?

'OK,' she said finally. 'Ring him—but I'll pay.'

He nodded, picked up the phone and left a message with Huw's secretary for him to call back, then replaced the phone in its cradle and drained his coffee—the fourth that morning. He was going to have a heart attack at this rate.

'I need to get on.'

'Me, too. How's Jacob?'

Reality. Thank God for reality. 'Good,' he replied. 'He's conscious and talking, and they're moving him to the high-dependency unit today. Looks like the brain injury may not be as serious as they'd feared, and his legs and pelvis are healing well, so hopefully he'll soon be up and about.'

Her smile lit up his world. 'I'm so pleased. Well done.'

'Thanks.' He didn't pretend false modesty. He knew he was a good surgeon, his high standards wouldn't allow him to be anything less, but her praise still warmed him, and he smiled back, stood up and pulled her into his arms and hugged her, unable to stop himself.

It felt so good to hold her. So right. And if Huw discovered that she *was* a carrier, then maybe…

'I have to go,' she murmured, snuggling closer and sighing.

He let her go and stepped back. 'Me, too.'

'Will I see you tonight?'

'Probably not. We're on take. I expect all hell will break loose. I'll give you a call when I hear from Huw—can I give him your mobile number?'

'Of course you can. I'll have it with me. And thank you.'

She reached up and kissed his cheek, then went back to the ward to check an IV line on a baby, and all the time she was working on him, then changing a dressing on another child, setting up an infusion in a child with Crohn's who was in for a few days to recover her strength before surgery to remove an obstruction in her bowel, doing the drugs round—through it all, she was waiting for Huw's call.

It came at lunchtime, after she'd done the discharge notes and said goodbye to Joel, who was going home to continue his convalescence, and as she went into the office to grab some lunch, her phone rang.

'Hi, it's Huw Parry. I gather you want to see me for DMD screening?'

'Yes, that's right,' she said, suddenly nervous as the reality of it hit her. 'I've been referred to you by the GP and I haven't heard anything, but it's not really urgent. I'm just getting a bit edgy, and Mr Langham-Jones suggested seeing you privately.'

'Are you busy now?'

'Now?' she squeaked, and swallowed. 'No, I'm not busy now. Nothing that can't wait, I'm on a break.'

'Can you come down? We can fill in a few forms, run through the questions and I can send off the bloods. Come to Medical Genetics and ask them to call me.'

'So how did it go?'

She pushed the cat off her lap and went to put the kettle on while she talked to him. She'd been waiting for him to ring for ages. 'Fine. He asked all sorts of questions, took a family history and about a gallon of blood and that was it, really. I already knew all the biology of inherited genes, the one in two chance of passing it on if I'm a carrier.'

'But only one in four of it affecting a child,' Andrew corrected.

'No. One in four that it's a boy with the disease, but also one in four that it's a girl who'll be a carrier, and as far as I'm concerned, that's affected, and pre-implantation genetic diagnosis wouldn't alter that. I'm not prepared to hand this bombshell on for my daughter to deal with when her time comes, any more than I want to give my son a life sentence. So, as far as I'm concerned, it's a one in two chance, even with screening, and that's crazy odds.'

She heard his good-natured sigh down the phone. 'OK, you win. One in two. So how long did he think it would take to get the results?'

'A couple of weeks. Maybe less, maybe more. There are several layers of testing. I feel sick now. I wish you were here.'

She heard him sigh. 'Me, too. I'm sorry, it's really busy. I've had a spate of little accidents—greenstick fractures, squashed fingers, a dislocated elbow. My registrar told me to go, but she's run off her feet and I don't like to make the children wait. I'll get over later if I can, just for a while.'

'Please do,' she said, suddenly realising how much she needed him there with her, how much she wanted to talk through what Huw Parry had told her.

Not that there was anything more to say, really, but somehow she just longed for the comfort of his presence, the warmth of his body hard up against hers, holding her while she waited.

Which was ridiculous, because it could be weeks, and he couldn't just be there and hold her for weeks, but so much hung in the balance. If she was a carrier, then she might—just might—be able to persuade him to give them a chance.

And perversely, having spent a year hoping she wasn't

a carrier, she now found herself hoping that she was, because the thought of life without him was extraordinarily painful, far more painful than the loss of any theoretical family she might have in the future.

Besides, there was always adoption.

She hugged her arms around herself, needing him, wishing he was there, and when he came to her at ten she went into his arms without a word and just held on.

# CHAPTER TEN

THE next two weeks were difficult, but as the days passed without a word from Huw Parry, Libby forced herself to put the results out of her mind and concentrate on the good things in her life.

Like Andrew, and her patients, who were fortunately keeping her busy. Jacob was doing well, up on his feet now and making slow, cautious progress with a frame—and of course Amy was up there, too, helping him walk again, his gait a little affected by the head injury but not so badly that he'd have any serious long-term issues.

And the trouble with Amy was that she saw too much.

'You look funny,' she said, getting straight to the point. 'What's going on, Libs?'

She looked away, her heart jerking against her ribs. 'Nothing. We've got some tricky patients at the moment. I'm just a bit distracted.'

Amy made a noncommittal noise, but Libby wasn't sharing her innermost fears and feelings with her friend. She was having enough trouble sharing them with Andrew, and he was involved.

Or possibly not, but she'd like him to be. He was still being cagey, though, a little distant, and she couldn't wait to get the results, but as the end of the second week came, she began to fret.

'Let's go away again,' Andrew said on Friday evening. 'Just for a night. There's a pub on the Thames, right down by the water. We could stay there—get right away.'

'Not Paris? Not a trick weekend like the last time you took me away?' she teased, and he chuckled.

'No. It's near Goring, on the Berkshire–Oxfordshire border. Why don't I ring them, see if they've got a room?'

They had, and she packed the next morning while Andrew went home and did the same, then he came back and picked her up and they set off, skirting London on the M25 and heading down into Berkshire.

'Good idea?' he said, locking the car and following her to the river bank at the edge of the car park.

'Lovely. It's so pretty—look, the weeping willows are trailing in the water, and there's a cherry flowering. Oh, and baby ducks! Oh, it's beautiful. Can we go for a walk?'

'Can we have lunch first?'

'I should think so,' she conceded with a smile, and they ordered sandwiches at the bar and ate them looking out over the river at the ducks and geese and moorhens, and then they went for a walk along the river's edge until they reached a fence and had to turn back.

She pulled a face. 'We can't get as far as I'd thought. Pity. I wanted to look at the houses.'

He chuckled. 'You want to snoop? We'll get a boat,' he said, and they went back to the pub and hired a little motor launch, and went upriver through the lock gates, gazing at all the houses—some modest, some outrageously ostentatious—whose gardens stretched down to the water's edge, and speculating laughingly on who lived in them. The ducks paddled hastily out of the way, and at one point they were joined by a swan which sailed majestically alongside, eyeing them with disdain.

And then at last, even wrapped up as warmly as they were, the chilly wind off the water got to them and they turned back, headed downstream to the pub and warmed up with a pot of tea and a slice of home-made gingerbread, snuggled together on a sofa by the fireside.

'This was a lovely idea,' she murmured, and he dropped a kiss on her hair and hugged her closer.

'Good. I'm glad you approve. It's a favourite haunt of Will and Sally's. They sneak down here every now and again for a bit of privacy, and apparently the restaurant's fabulous.'

'I'll need to work up a bit of an appetite if we're having dinner,' she said, staring at the empty plate in dismay. 'I only meant to eat a tiny piece of that. I'm getting fatter by the minute.'

He nuzzled her ear. 'Rubbish. You're gorgeous.'

'Andrew, you're feeding me constantly!' she protested. 'I swear my clothes are tighter.'

'Gorgeous,' he repeated, his eyes smouldering behind the smile. 'Are you finished with that tea? We need to dress for dinner,' he added, confusing her.

'Dinner? It's only five o'clock, and, anyway, it's a pub!'

'You're still going to need to dress for dinner,' he murmured. 'Unless you want to shock the other diners? You did say something about working up an appetite…'

'Andrew!' she whispered, scandalised and horribly tempted, a giggle bubbling in her throat as he got to his feet and held out his hand, a lazy, sensuous challenge in his eyes.

She took it.

Going away for the weekend was all very well, but on Sunday night reality came crashing back. She was alone again, Andrew as usual going home to attend to paperwork and catch up with his work, and the wait for the results was tearing her into little pieces.

She met him for coffee the next morning, after a sleepless and wretched night, and he frowned at her and touched the shadows under her eyes with a warm, blunt fingertip.

'You look tired.'

'I didn't sleep. Andrew, I don't think I can stand this waiting any longer, but I can't bring myself to ring Huw Parry and every time my phone rings I feel sick.'

He searched her eyes, pulled her gently into his arms and hugged her. 'Do you want me to ring?' he offered, holding his breath, because the truth was the wait was getting to him, too, and he wanted it over every bit as much as Libby clearly did.

'Would you?'

'Sure.'

He used his desk phone, switching it to hands-free, and called Huw's secretary.

'Hi, it's Andrew Langham-Jones here. Could you see if you've got the test results for Elizabeth Tate, please? She was having bloods and screening for DMD.'

'Yes, sure, of course.' They heard her flicking through files, the rustle of paper, and then the scrape as she picked up the phone again.

'Um, we haven't got the dystrophin gene result back, but the bloods are here: the creatine phosphokinase is normal and the pregnancy test was positive.'

His world ground to a halt, until even the clock seemed to stop ticking, and he met Libby's stunned eyes in confusion. Pregnant? Libby was *pregnant*?

'No!' she mouthed, the blood draining from her face, and he felt sick. She couldn't be—not unless...

'Hello?'

'Um—hi. Yeah. Thanks. Um—tell Huw I'll call him, could you?'

'Sure. I'm going off now, but I'll leave a note for him, Mr Langham-Jones. Thank you.'

The dial tone buzzed loudly in the room, and he reached out an unsteady hand to press the 'off' button and met Libby's distraught eyes.

'Libby, I—'

'I can't be pregnant,' she said softly. 'Oh, Andrew, I can't be! How?'

'I have no idea. I can't—' he began, and Libby leapt to her feet, twisting her hands together, her mouth open, her breath jerking in and out of tortured lungs.

'Well, apparently you can. Oh, I can't believe I've been so *stupid*! I *knew* you hadn't had proper tests, I *knew* there was a risk—you even bought condoms, for goodness' sake! Why on earth didn't I let you use them? I must have been crazy! Oh, dear God, Andrew, what on earth are we going to do?'

He got to his feet, his legs shaking, and walked over to her, resting his hand gently on her shoulder. 'Libby, I'm so sorry. If I'd had the slightest idea—the merest *hint* that there was any possibility I could get you pregnant, do you imagine for a *moment* that I would have made love to you without using protection?'

She shook her head. 'It's not your fault, it's mine. I knew how important it was not to get pregnant with this hanging over me, but I did nothing about it, and I should have done. You *know* how I feel about it, about the prospect of conceiving a child who might be—'

She broke off, pressing her fists to her mouth, her eyes wild with grief and anger and despair, and the fleeting, momentary doubt that it could be his child was banished in that instant, replaced by the absolute certainty that he was the father.

He wasn't infertile. He had been, he was sure of that, but apparently not any longer. And now the woman he loved more than anyone else in the world was carrying his child.

And that child might have inherited a dreadful, life-limiting disease because he hadn't followed up his test results properly, just assumed that the situation hadn't changed.

'Libby, I'm so sorry,' he began again, but she drew herself up and away from him, her arms hugging her waist, her eyes tortured.

'Sorry isn't the point, Andrew. We're both sorry, but this is one thing that being sorry isn't going to change. I'm having a baby who may or may not be going to die after years of suffering, and it's my fault. Your fault, too, for not double-checking, but my fault for believing you, and only I knew the significance of an unplanned pregnancy. Why on earth did I do that?' she asked, a trifle hysterically. 'I'm not stupid, I know things can change. I should have insisted we used protection.'

He rammed his hands through his hair, his emotions knotting his stomach. 'Libby, I'm so sorry, but I really was so sure. I did the tests. Again and again.'

'But years ago, Andrew! And you said yourself you'd been ill. And when I asked if you'd had it checked by anyone recently, you said what's the point, either they're there swimming or they're not. And I didn't even question it, and I should have done.'

'I really believed it. It must have been a blip, but it went on so long—years. It was several years after I found out that I looked again, and, believe me, Libby, there was nothing.'

'Well, there obviously isn't nothing now, and you need

to know that this is your child, so can I suggest that you go and get checked out?'

'Why? I have no intention of wriggling out of my responsibility,' he said quietly, tortured by guilt, reeling from the utterly unexpected news that he could have fathered a child. 'In fact, I have every intention of being there for our child on a daily basis, starting with marrying you.'

'Marrying me?' she said, her voice dropping to a shocked whisper. 'Why would you do that? You didn't sign up for this—for a disabled child.'

'You're getting ahead of yourself. It's only one in four.'

'That's pretty good odds if it was a lottery ticket,' she said. 'And, anyway, there's no way I'm marrying you. Not now you know you can have children with anyone you like. Maybe even Cousin Charlotte,' she added, and blinking back a fresh wave of tears, she yanked open the door and ran out, leaving him standing there, rooted to the spot, his thoughts in turmoil.

He wasn't sterile.

It had dominated his life, governed his every move, every relationship, every day that he spent with children. And it was no longer true.

He was going to be a father, and what should have been the happiest day of his life was turning into a potential tragedy.

He closed the door softly, sat on the edge of the desk and stared blankly at the wall. Please, let it be a girl, he prayed. Don't let this child be stricken. Not my baby. Our baby. It's done nothing wrong.

There was a sharp rap on the door, and he swallowed hard. 'Yes?'

'It's only me. Hell, what on earth's happened?'

Andrew met his brother's shocked, searching eyes and swallowed hard.

'Libby's pregnant,' he managed.

'What?'

'Shut the door. There's a problem.'

'A problem?' He shut the door, his eyes piercing. 'What sort of problem, apart from her being pregnant? Don't tell me—she's demanding you marry her?'

'Actually, I asked her, and she turned me down. Suggested I ask Cousin Charlotte.'

Will's jaw dropped, and he sat down on the edge of the desk and frowned. 'Wow. Are you sure it's yours?'

He gave a startled laugh. 'Oh, yes. If you'd seen her face—you can't fake that kind of reaction. This is my child, I know it is, because I know she wouldn't expose herself to the risk of pregnancy at the moment and she didn't realise there was a risk, because I told her—oh, hell, you might as well know. I thought I was sterile.'

His brother's eyes widened. 'What? What on earth gave you that idea?'

So he told him, and Will stared at him in horror. 'And you never mentioned it? Hell, is this why you won't get involved with anyone?' He nodded, and Will scrubbed a hand through his hair. 'So—you thought you couldn't get her pregnant, so you didn't use anything?'

He nodded again. 'Only apparently I can, and did. And here's the problem. She's being screened for DMD—Duchenne muscular dystrophy. Her sister's a carrier.'

Will's jaw dropped, and he blew out his breath on a soft sigh. 'Oh, my God.'

'Yeah. So, the good news is I'm going to be a father. The bad new is—'

'Hey, stop. It's only a one in four.'

'Only?' he said drily. 'Or one in two, if you ask Libby.

She doesn't want a daughter, either, if she's got the gene. She's adamant about not passing it on to a future generation.'

'She wouldn't…'

Pain sliced through him, and he had to force himself to breathe. 'I have no idea. I hope not, but she won't talk to me, and she said she wouldn't marry me.'

And suddenly it all got too much for him, and a choking sob rose in his throat. He pressed his fist to his mouth, but his chest heaved and he found himself wrapped hard in his brother's arms, held tight while the waves of pain and shock ripped through him, leaving him empty. Gutted.

'You need to go home,' Will said softly as he pulled away and dragged his hands over his face.

'I can't. I've got work to do.'

'Then have a coffee, and sit and talk this through with me for a while, because there's no way you're going any-where in this state,' Will said firmly, and, pushing him down into his chair, he handed him a mug and then perched opposite, elbows propped on the desk, studying him.

'You need to talk to her, bro'.'

He shook his head. 'She walked out. She needs time, Will. I have to give her time—time to calm down, to think it through. And I need time, too. It's just so much to take in, and there's a bit of me that's trying to be happy because it means we can be together and raise a family, but the rest of me—'

He clamped his teeth together, fighting back another wave of grief for the child who might have been handed a life sentence by his careless assumptions. 'I'm a doctor, for God's sake! I should have known better. I should have checked, been properly investigated, not just assumed I knew enough to take that kind of risk. And now it's too late, and, as Libby said, this is one time when sorry isn't the point.'

'So what are you going to do?'

He scrubbed his hands through his hair and met Will's worried eyes.

'I have no idea. I really have no idea. But I'm not taking no for an answer.'

Libby didn't know how she found her way back to the ward.

She wouldn't have gone back there at all, but her bag was there with her car keys in it, and she had to hand over the ward to someone. And, of course, as luck would have it, the first person she saw was Amy.

Dear, sweet Amy, who took one look at her, shoved her into the office and shut the door.

'Libby? What's happened? Is it your sister? Your mother? Andrew?'

She shook her head, the tears she'd held back until now fighting their way to the surface, and Amy gave a soft cry and wrapped her in her arms, rocking her gently as she wept, one hand clamped over her mouth to stifle the great raw sobs tearing through her.

She couldn't tell Amy, couldn't share anything this personal, this agonising, because just to say the words out loud would make it real, and she was hoping, so desperately hoping that it would all go away.

Except, of course, it wouldn't.

'Oh, Libby!' Amy crooned softly. 'It's all right. It'll be all right.'

Oh, if only! Fresh tears scalded her cheeks, and she eased away, rummaging for a tissue with trembling fingers, blotting hopelessly at the tears which fell faster than she could catch them, as Amy steered her to a chair and sat her down, holding her still, stroking her face and murmuring softly to her.

'Is it Andrew? What's happened?'

She shook her head, pressing her fingers to her eyes until they ached, until everything went black, but she could still see his shocked face, the pain and confusion in his eyes as he came to terms with the fact that he was no longer sterile, and what that might now mean.

He wasn't the only one who was shocked and confused, though. She couldn't think clearly yet, needed time to let the news she'd never expected to hear sink in. Of all the random, cruel twists of fate, this was the one she might least have expected.

Of course it was, or she would have taken steps to ensure it could never have happened. Oh, how could she have been so stupid?

'I need to go home, Amy,' she said, battening down the tears and dragging out her self-control. 'Can you get someone to take over for me? There are some kids on the ward I was about to go and assess for discharge. Andr-Andrew's got the details.'

She got her bag out of the drawer and headed for the door, but Amy blocked her way.

'Libby, you can't drive like this.'

'I'll be fine.'

'At least tell me what's going on.'

She stared at her, her friend and yet not quite confidante, and shook her head. 'I can't. I will, but not now, please. Just let me go.'

Amy stepped out of the way, and Libby fled, running out to the car park, getting into her car and putting the key in the ignition with hands that were shaking so badly she could scarcely hold it.

Seat belt, she thought, clipping it, and drove home, blinking hard to keep the road in view. She shouldn't be driving. She knew that, but she had to get away, to get home, to crawl into bed and shut her eyes and wait for the pain to ease.

If it ever did…

'Libby's gone home.'

'Good. You should, too. Come back to mine.'

'No. I can't face the family.'

'Then I'll come to you, but you're not doing this alone,' Will said, and Andrew gave up. He'd been there for Will a thousand times, and they knew each other inside out.

'OK. I'll come to yours. Where are you now?'

'In the car park—I was just about to go. I'll wait for you.'

'Will, I'm fine.'

Will said something rude and to the point, and Andrew dropped his phone on the desk and rang through to his secretary.

'I'm knocking off early—bit of a headache. Could you make sure the team knows? If there's an emergency, I'm sure Patrick Corrigan will cover me. He's on take today.'

'Sure, Andrew. Can I get you anything?'

A miracle? Or had they already had that?

Be careful what you wish for, he thought, and swallowed hard. 'No, I'm fine, Janet, thank you. I'll see you tomorrow.'

He grabbed his coat and headed out of the building, lifting a hand in acknowledgement as Will's Land Rover pulled up near his car and waited, engine running. His kid brother, crazy, reckless, always in trouble; he'd bailed him out so many times.

Maybe it was time to let him return the favour.

She cried for hours, curled up in her bed, rocking to comfort herself, her arms wrapped firmly over the still-flat abdomen that cradled her baby.

'Please, God, let my baby be all right,' she wept brokenly. 'Please be a girl. Please don't let me have passed this on!'

She couldn't lie there any longer, couldn't do nothing, but there was nothing to do, nothing to say, nowhere she could go to escape the agonising wait for an answer to her questions. She'd have to wait for the results to come back, for the examination of the dystrophin gene to be painstakingly completed. And in the meantime, she had to stop crying and try and rationalise her behaviour, so she got out of bed and went downstairs, made herself a cup of tea and curled up on the sofa with Kitty.

And then thought about the risk to a pregnancy from cat litter and began to cry again. Even her cat was out of bounds, she thought, tears cascading down her cheeks.

She needed Andrew. She'd never needed anyone so much, but she'd shut him out, implied that he'd let her down, but he hadn't. She knew—had always known—that he was a good man, that there wasn't a lying, deceitful bone in his body, that for all he might have been mistaken, he'd made an honest, genuine mistake, and he was every bit as shocked and distressed by it as she was.

She had to ring him.

She found her phone, checked for messages, then hesitated. Wouldn't he have rung her if he'd cared? Really cared, rather than being dutiful? Chris Turner had told her he would have given up everything to look after Will had it been necessary. He was that sort of man.

Did she want that?

No. No, of course not, but he'd told her in Paris that he loved her.

Only not today. Today, he'd just told her was going to marry her and be involved in their child's life, and she'd told him to go and marry Cousin Charlotte. So why would he call her? She had to call him, to apologise. Fingers shaking, she dialled his number and waited till it went to the answering-machine.

Then she rang his house phone, with the same result.

He might be in the shower, or still at work—that was it. He'd be at work.

She rang the switchboard, asked them to page him, and was told he'd left the hospital at four.

Four? He never left at four. It was rare for him to leave before six, and often it was later than that. But he had left, and he wasn't answering her calls. Which could well be because he was in the shower she told herself, trying to be rational. He always showered when he got home from work.

She tried again later, both phones, and then at two in the morning she pulled on her coat and drove to his house, to find it deserted. No car, no lights.

Of course. He'd gone to Ashenden, gone to Will.

She had Will's number in her phone, and she hesitated, her finger hovering over the button, but then she threw it in her bag and drove home, a sick feeling in the pit of her stomach.

He'd asked her to marry him and she just walked out, refusing to discuss it. Why should he want to talk to her?

She went inside, threw her bag down on the sofa, went to bed and cried herself to sleep a little before dawn.


'I ought to ring her.'

'Really? You're drunk, Andrew.'

'I know. But I still ought to ring her—damn! Where's my mobile?'

'I don't know. When did you last have it?'

'In my office—oh, hell. She might have been trying me, and I don't know her number.'

'I've got her mobile number,' Will said, 'but it is three in the morning. She's probably asleep.'

'No. She'll be churning it over in her mind, and I ought to be with her. I should have been with her all the time.Give me the number, I'll ring her.'

Will threw his phone across to him, and he rang her.

Three times.

Each time it rang and rang, then went to the answering-machine, but he didn't say anything, just hung up. He had no idea what to say; he needed to hear her voice, get some feedback, before he could launch in and say anything.

And she wasn't answering her phone to him.

He dropped the phone in despair and stared at Will.

'OK. You're the expert. What the hell do I do now?'

Will smiled a little crookedly. 'You go to bed, sleep off that brandy and I'll wake you up and take you to work. Got a clean shirt there?'

He nodded. He always had a full set of clean clothes at work, because you never knew when accidents might happen, especially working with children.

Children. He didn't want to think about children. Sick children, children with life-limiting conditions, children who were sick and going downhill and all you could do was slow the progress...

'I can drive myself.'

'No, you can't. You've been drinking, you'll probably be hovering on the limit.'

'So have you.'

'Not like you. And I hope you aren't operating?'

He shook his head. 'No. Clinics.' Clinics with children. Sick children...

Will eyed him thoughtfully. 'Actually, of course, there's only a one in eight chance,' Will said, reading his mind.

'What?'

'You don't know if Libby's a carrier. That's a one in two. That halves the odds. Or doubles them. Don't know which I mean, but it makes it one in eight, not one in four, that it's an affected boy.'

One in eight.

Better, but no way good enough to comfort him.

'I love her,' he said conversationally. 'And she loves me. Why aren't we together now, Will, talking this through?'

'Because it's three in the morning and she's upset? She'll calm down and think it through.'

'I don't think so. What the hell am I going to do if she won't listen to me?' He stood up and headed for the door. 'I'm going to bed. Wake me at six. Maybe it'll look better then.'

It was a forlorn hope.

Will dropped him at work at seven-thirty, and he went straight up to his office and found his phone lying there on the desk.

With two missed calls from Libby. He checked the time of her calls, late last night, and cursed the fact that he'd been stupid enough to leave his phone behind. Stupid enough to drink, so he couldn't just get in the car and drive round to her house and bang on the door and demand to talk to her.

Stupid enough to make assumptions, to rely on his clearly flawed judgement and make a colossal mistake with potentially massive consequences.

Hands shaking, he rang her, and got her answering-machine…

## CHAPTER ELEVEN

She had missed calls on her mobile.

Three, from Will. Nothing from Andrew.

She didn't want to talk to Will, didn't know what to say to him. Did he know? Had Andrew spoken to him?

Or maybe, she thought as a chill ran over her, maybe something had happened to him. She checked the time of the calls. After three in the morning. Oh, lord. Was Andrew hurt? Sick? What if he'd had an accident?

She ran through the shower, slapped on some make-up to cover the ravages of the night and drove to work. She'd go and see if he was in his office, leave him a note. Check with the ED to see if he'd been brought in.

No. She wouldn't even let herself think about that until she'd checked his office, she thought, and hurried through the hospital, along the corridor to his office outside the paediatric ward. Her hand was raised to knock when the door swung inwards, and he stood there, looking like she felt, his eyes red-rimmed, his mouth set in a grim line, his cheeks sunken with exhaustion.

He was all right. Not in Emergency, or undergoing surgery, not in ITU linked up to a million machines. Just screening her calls. She felt sick, but she lifted her chin and met his eyes.

'Andrew, we need to talk,' she said, and he stepped back and let her in, then closed the door.

'I'm sorry.'

They spoke together, and then with a muffled groan he reached for her, hauling her into his arms and holding her close.

'I tried to ring you, but you didn't answer, and you weren't at home,' she mumbled into his shirt.

'Will took me home, and I forgot my phone. I tried to ring you on his.'

Will's phone. The missed calls. He *had* tried to ring her.

'I thought—I was so awful to you.'

'I deserved it,' he said quietly. 'I've behaved like an idiot. You were right, I should have checked. No wonder you hate me.'

'I don't hate you,' she cut in, tilting her head up so she could see his eyes. Tortured, tormented eyes. 'I just don't know if I want to marry you—not under these circumstances. You're a good man, Andrew, I know that. And I know you really thought you couldn't have children, but I'm scared and I just don't know—I don't know where to go from here.'

His hands gripped her arms reassuringly.

'Nor do I, but one thing I do know—we do it together. I love you, Libby, and you love me, and this is our baby. Whatever the outcome, whatever the consequences, this is our child, and we'll do this together. Marry me.'

Libby shook her head.

'Andrew, I can't! Not now, not like this! It's not a sound basis for a marriage.'

'Rubbish. We love each other, Libby. We have done right from the start. I've loved you since you told my brother he was a better dancer than me.'

She gave a strangled laugh. 'Maybe he is?'

'No, he's not. You were being generous—as usual. And I shouldn't have taken advantage of you that night."

'You didn't,' she corrected softly. 'I needed you so much. Needed to reach out with my hands, to touch you—I'd been falling for you for ages, but I didn't think you'd even noticed me until you asked me to go home with you for the weekend. So you didn't take advantage of me—if anything I took advantage of you. And it's not your fault I'm pregnant. I've known about this DMD for a year. I should have made sure I couldn't get pregnant, not just relied on my relentlessly single status.'

'That's my line.' He smiled, a little crookedly, then shook his head. 'I still don't see why you won't marry me.'

'Because it's not why you get married.'

'So why do you get married? If it's not because you're with the person you love, and you're having a baby together, and then you find out something might mean your child needs even more care, more love, and you'll need each other more than ever before—what better basis could there be, Libby?'

She shook her head. 'You didn't want to get married.'

'Of course I did! I've always wanted to get married and settle down, but I didn't want to trap a woman into a childless marriage and find out years down the line that loving me wasn't enough! You knew that. If it hadn't been for my infertility, I would have asked you to marry me in Paris.'

'And I would have said no, at least until I'd had the tests.'

'Why? Why do you imagine it would make any difference to me? I love you, Libby—you, not our children. If you'd decided not to have any, I would have been fine with that.'

'Would you? So why is it all right for you to decide to sacrifice your chance of being a parent, but not for me?'

He frowned. 'Because I'd know. I'd make the decision, stick to it, and know I could make it work for us.'

'But you couldn't have trusted me to do the same?'

He closed his eyes with a sigh. 'I couldn't have *asked* you to do that for me.'

'Well, it's not relevant now, anyway, is it? The fact is your fertility is not an issue. The issue is my carrier status, and I need to know the answer before I can give you one.'

'No. It won't make any difference to me, Libby. At the very least, we're having this one child, whatever the results of your test, and we love each other, and we'll love the child, and the greater that child's needs, the more important it is that we do this together. I can't cope with this without you, Libby. I need you. I'm not coming and spending time with my disabled son and then going home at night and leaving you to cope, if that's the way this turns out. No way. And if the baby's fine, if you're not a carrier or it's unaffected, then there's no reason not to be together. Not when we love each other so much. Is there?'

She searched his eyes, seeing only love and confusion and pain, but no doubt. Not a shred, not a trace of any doubt.

'No. No, there's no reason not to be together, and I can't do this without you, either,' she admitted softly.

'So you will marry me?'

She hesitated. This wasn't what she'd expected, what she'd dreamed of. That night in Paris, if he'd asked her then—or down in Berkshire on Saturday, maybe. But now? For expediency?

'I don't want to rush you,' he said softly. 'You obviously need to think about this.'

'No. I don't need to think about it. I love you, of course I do. I just wish…' She trailed off, and he sighed.

'So do I, but we don't have the luxury of choice. So is that a yes?'

She nodded. 'Yes, Andrew, it's a yes,' she said, and burst into tears.

He gathered her up against his heart, wishing he could make it different for her, for all of them, but he couldn't, so he just held her, unable to make any promises bar the one that he would love her for the rest of his life.

'Hey, come on,' he murmured. 'You're soaking me and I don't have another shirt here.'

She laughed, a strange, hiccuping little laugh, and let him go. 'You'd better phone Will, he'll be worried.'

'Yes. Look, I've got a lot to do today—will you be all right now?'

She nodded. 'I'll be fine. Can we talk tonight?'

'Sure. My car's at Ashenden. Will drove me in. I hit the brandy a bit—can you drive me out there and we'll tell my parents?'

Her eyes widened in what looked like panic. 'Really?'

'Really. And I want to marry you soon—as soon as I can. There's no going back on this for me, Libby, I want you to know that. I'll find out what the rules are and let you know. OK?'

She nodded, and went up on tiptoe and kissed his freshly shaved and slightly nicked cheek. 'You've cut yourself,' she murmured, and he fingered the little slice in his jaw and smiled.

'Yeah. Must have been thinking about something else. I'll see you later—give me a call when you finish.'

Amy was waiting for her, and her face lit up with relief.

'Oh, Libby, I've been so worried! I was going to ring you, but—are you OK?'

'I'm fine,' she said, dredging up a rather weary smile for her friend. 'I'm sorry I worried you. I was just…' She trailed off, not knowing how to explain without giving all the details, the thought that she was to marry Andrew still filtering through to her exhausted and emotionally drained mind.

'What on earth happened?' Amy asked. 'You looked so awful—I thought someone had died.'

She shook her head. 'No. It was just…'

Amy waited, then smiled. 'It's OK. Tell me when you're ready, but if you need to talk, or a shoulder to cry on, just yell.'

'Actually, I do,' she said, her eyes welling up again. 'Can we do coffee later? I've got so much to tell you, and I don't really know where to start.'

'Better make it lunch, then,' Amy suggested with a wry smile. 'My treat.'

Amy sat in silence while Libby explained, and for once there wasn't the slightest hint of eager anticipation, just a quiet watchfulness that made Libby realise she'd underestimated Amy all along.

'So—how pregnant are you?' she asked eventually, when Libby ground to a halt.

'I don't know. It could have been anything up to four weeks ago.'

'Four—but that must have been the weekend of the birthday!'

She nodded. 'I didn't really know Andrew before the weekend, but I'd been so aware of him since I first met him, and suddenly there we were together, having an amazing time, and—well, it just happened. And we've been together ever since.'

'Wow. I thought you looked different, but I didn't realise

how different. And then you decided to go for the test. Why? Why then?'

'Because we realised we were falling in love, and—you can't go into a relationship with that kind of uncertainty.'

'But you're going to marry him now?'

'Yes.'

'And not just for the baby?'

She shook her head and smiled. 'No, not just for the baby. I love him, Amy. He's a wonderful person, and he makes me laugh, and he makes me happy. But I'm so scared for the baby.'

Amy shook her head. 'Don't be. There are so many more treatments these days, and it's still possible to have a good and meaningful life with DMD. OK, it's progressive and there's nothing you can do about that, but there may be, in time. There might be some way of stopping the muscle wasting in the future, and with a paediatric nurse and an orthopaedic surgeon for parents, how could he do better? You'll be brilliant parents, whatever the future holds for your baby—and, anyway, you might not even be a carrier, so you could be worrying yourself sick for nothing.'

All of which she knew, but it still preyed at the back of her mind all day, and when she picked Andrew up at five-thirty she was feeling sick with exhaustion and emotion.

'Do you really want to talk to your parents tonight?' she asked, and he nodded.

'We won't be long. I'll pick my car up and we'll go back to my house, OK, and talk it all through?'

She nodded. 'We need to feed Kitty now, then,' she said, and they did that on their way to Ashenden.

Will was crossing the stableyard as they pulled in, and he came over to them, smiling warily.

'Hi. Everything OK?' he asked, and Andrew gave a soft laugh and hugged her to his side.

'Yes. Everything's OK. I've asked Libby to marry me, and she's said yes.'

Will's eyes swivelled to hers, and his smile widened, lighting up his eyes as he reached for them and hugged them both, slapping Andrew on the back and laughing.

'Excellent. Go and tell the parents, they'll be overjoyed.'

'You haven't said anything?'

'What—and steal your thunder? I should think not. Go on, go and tell them the glad tidings, and I'll fetch Sally and we'll come and have a drink with you in a minute.'

'I'm not drinking,' Andrew said wryly, and with Will's chuckle echoing in their ears, they turned and went into the house.


'Andrew, Libby! How nice to see you! You should have said you were coming, I could have cooked for you.'

'It's fine. We'll eat later. Actually, we've got something to tell you. Can we sit down?'

His mother's eyes missed nothing, scanning them both before returning to his face. 'Does this need the drawing room, or will the kitchen do?'

'I would have thought the kitchen would be fine,' he said with a smile, and beside him he felt Libby relax a little. 'Put the kettle on, Mum, and come and sit down.'

They settled round the table, and he told them, in edited terms, the good news and the bad news, in that order.

His mother's face crumpled briefly, and then she stood up and came to Libby and hugged her tenderly. 'Sweetheart, I'm so sorry, but we're here for you, whatever the result of this, and if there's anything we can do to help, in any way, at any time, then you must ask. Please, promise me you'll ask.'

'I promise,' she said, touched to her heart by this woman's compassionate kindness and warmth. 'And I'm sorry it's a little unconventional.'

Jane flapped her hand and smiled. 'Andrew was "early",' she said with a chuckle. 'You aren't the first and you won't be the last, and we couldn't have had a better, stronger, more loving marriage. So—when's the wedding?'

'As soon as possible,' Andrew said firmly. 'We haven't talked about the sort of wedding we want, but we do agree on that, don't we? Don't we?'

He shot her a questioning glance, and she nodded, suddenly sure that this was the right thing to do, even though the result was still hanging over them, because this was no longer about some theoretical question but about a real baby, and a real love.

'Yes, we do,' she said, just as firmly. 'I don't know what Andrew wants, but I'd like a quiet church wedding, if possible. My mother and her husband are in Ireland, and my sister's in Cumbria with her husband and her little girl, but apart from them and Amy and a few others who I work with, there isn't really anyone much. A few old friends from when I was training, that's all.'

Jane was settling down with a notepad and pen.

'Right. The four of us, Libby, Sally, Libby's mother and stepfather, Libby's sister and husband and daughter, Amy, Chris and Louise Turner—you met them at the party, our GP.'

She nodded. 'Yes. I liked him. Isn't his wife the vicar?'

'Yes, which is really handy. Anyone else?'

'Not imperative, no,' Andrew said. 'Of course there's always Cousin Charlotte…'

The mischievous twinkle was back in his tired, red-rimmed eyes, and Libby chuckled.

'Poor Cousin Charlotte. She'll be heartbroken.'

'She will—you're unkind to her, Andrew,' his mother chided gently.

'She's fixated. She needs to get over herself. How many is that?'

'Fourteen.'

Libby nodded. 'That sounds OK—oh my neighbours. He's been really good to me and she's lovely. Oh, and there's a cousin, Edward,' she added, looking up at Andrew. 'I met him at the funeral. I don't know if he'll be able to come. He may not be well enough.'

'We'll ask him,' Andrew said gently.

'That's seventeen. I'm sure there will be a few more, but we'll keep it under twenty,' Jane promised. 'Leave it to me. I'll find out when the church is free—fifteen clear days, isn't it? Or three Sundays? Does it have to be a Saturday?'

'Any day suits me, I don't mind,' Andrew said. 'I'll book it off as soon as we've agreed a date with the church.'

'I'll phone Louise now and find out the technicalities,' Tony said, getting to his feet. 'Andrew? Could we have a word?'

They left the room, and Jane looked up from her list and smiled. 'I'm so glad it's you. I really wondered if he'd ever settle down. I had no idea about the fertility issue. I wonder what made him check it?'

Libby had no intention of discussing that with his mother, but it was a rhetorical question, the woman who'd given birth to him and raised him much more concerned with the impact it had had on his life.

'You know, I always felt there was something wrong, but I couldn't put my finger on it,' she murmured. 'I mean, he's always been so strong on family, so loyal and dutiful, and I know he grumbles about this old place, but he loves it, really, and I know it'll be in safe hands when we're gone.' She met Libby's eyes.

'You do realise, I take it, that you'll be Lady Ashenden when that happens?' she said gently, and Libby felt her mouth open.

'Oh, good grief, I hadn't given it a moment's thought,' she said, panic washing over her. 'I can't possibly—'

'Can't possibly what? Love my son and raise your children here in this lovely, draughty old house? Of course you can, my dear. It's a wonderful place for children, just a great big adventure playground. And, anyway, we have no intention of handing over the reins for years, so relax and enjoy yourself and worry about it when we get carted off in a box.'

'Who's getting carted off in a box?' Tony asked, coming back in with Andrew, and Jane laughed.

'Nobody, yet. So what did Louise say?'

'We can be married here in the chapel so long as there's a registrar attending, because we don't have our own register, and we'll need a notice of marriage, so provided we do that first thing tomorrow, we can be married here two weeks on Friday.'

By which time, she thought, her heart pounding, she would know the answer. Even though it wouldn't change anything, she wanted Andrew to know what he was taking on—the fact, not the possibility. Suddenly, perhaps because she'd been reminded of Edward and his abrupt exit from her life, that had assumed a greater importance.

'Two weeks on Friday sounds fine.'

'Right. Libby, you may have your own ideas, but—I'd be so pleased if you'd let me do your flowers.'

Flowers? She hadn't even thought about flowers, but it suddenly came home to her in a rush that she was getting married, to a man she loved with all her heart, and his family were welcoming her with open arms.

'Thank you, that would be lovely,' she said, her eyes filling, and as she and Jane stood up and hugged, Will walked into the room with Sally, and they grinned.

'I take it you aren't being disinherited, then, bro'? Never mind,' Will said, and they all laughed, but Andrew's arm slid round her and hugged her close, and she knew that whatever happened, whatever fate had in store for them, it would be all right, because they'd have each other…

He eventually got her away from the family and back to his house.

'I'm exhausted,' she said. 'Don't cook, I only want a bit of toast.'

'OK. There's something I want to say to you first, though, and I know it's a bit cock-eyed and back to front, but…' He swallowed hard, feeling suddenly ridiculously uncertain, and, taking her hand, he knelt down in front of her on one knee and stared up into her bemused, strained, beautiful eyes.

'I want you to forget everything except us,' he began. 'Because this is about us, and about nothing and no one else. I love you, Libby. It started when you were dancing with Will and I was so jealous of him, and it hit me like a truck in Paris. I've tried to rationalise it, tried to talk myself out of it, and I can't. I love you, really love you, and it's a love that won't go away, won't fade, won't weary. I want to watch you grow old, I want to see you with grey hair and wrinkles, still smiling at me over breakfast, still loving me back the way you do now.

'I want to be with you for the rest of my life, for better, for worse, for richer, for poorer, in sickness and in health. I need you. You're my other half, and I know I said I was never going to marry, but I can't imagine how much it would have hurt me to let you go, or how I would have done it.

'I know I'm crabby sometimes, and I'll probably get a lot worse as I get older, and it means you'll end up living in a heap of dry rot some day, but I swear I will do everything I can to make you and our children happy, and to care for you, if you'll do me the honour of being my wife. Will you, Libby? Will you marry me?'

She stared down at him, her eyes filling until his dear, beloved face was just a blur, and then she knelt down in front of him and went into his arms.

'Oh, Andrew—of course I'll marry you! I can't think of anything I want or need more than to be with you for ever. Of course I'll marry you. I'd be honoured.'

He hugged her, then released her gently and put his hand into his pocket, pulling out a ring.

A beautiful ring, three diamonds in a row in a simple, antique setting, which he slid onto her finger. 'It was my great-grandmother's ring,' he said softly. 'I didn't know if it would even fit you, but it can be altered if necessary.'

But it wasn't. It fitted perfectly, sparkling through her tears, and bringing fresh ones that welled up and spilled over. 'Oh, Andrew, it's beautiful!' she whispered. 'Oh, thank you!'

'You'll have to give it back one day,' he said with a wry smile, 'when our son's getting married.'

And then she remembered, remembered that if they had a son, he might not ever live to marry, and her tears fell again, mingling with his as they held each other tight and hung on.

'I can't zip my dress up—honestly, I can't believe how much my bust has grown!'

'Let me—there. You look fabulous,' Amy said, standing back and grinning broadly. 'Fantastic. You'll knock his socks off. Doesn't she look great?'

Libby's mother nodded, then her eyes filled with tears and she hugged her daughter gently. 'You look absolutely beautiful, darling. Gorgeous. He's a lucky man.'

Oh, lord, I hope so, she thought.

There was still no news. The clinic was open, she could ring Huw Parry, but she didn't want to, not now, not so close to the wedding.

The results were taking for ever, and she'd been so sure they would have been back in time, but they weren't, and in an hour's time she was marrying Andrew with the uncertainty still hanging over them.

'Is that your mobile? I'll fetch it.'

Her heart crashed against her ribs, and she took the phone from Amy as she ran back upstairs with it, staring at the number in consternation.

It was Huw.

'Who's ringing you?'

'God knows.' He pulled his phone out of his pocket and stared at it. 'Libby.' He flipped it open. 'Hi, darling, what's up? Libby? Libby, for God's sake, talk to me.'

'I've got the results,' she said, and then started to cry again, incoherent.

He shut the phone and stared at Will. 'She's got the results. I'm going over there.'

'Not on your own, you're not. I'll drive you.'

For once he was glad that Will had no fear and that there was no traffic on the road—and apparently no police. They pulled up outside her house and he was out of the car before it stopped, running up her path and pounding on the door.

'Libby! Let me in!'

The door opened and she fell into his arms, her face awash with tears. 'Oh, Andrew!' she wailed, and sobbed into his shirt front.

'What?' he demanded, freeing himself and holding her at arm's length, desperately trying to work out what she was saying, but she was laughing and crying so hard he couldn't understand a word.

'I'm not a carrier,' she managed finally, but by then he'd worked it out from the laughter and the smiles of the women grouped around behind her, and Will slapping him on the back, and the huge ball of pain that had been lodged in his chest for the last few weeks dissolved, leaving nothing but a searing joy so great it threatened to overwhelm him.

'Oh, my love,' he said brokenly. Dragging her into his arms, they wrapped her hard against his heart and held her while he wept.

'Um, you're not supposed to see your wife on your wedding day until the ceremony,' Will pointed out, shoving a handkerchief in his hand when he eventually let her go. 'It's unlucky.'

'No way,' he said, shaking his head and smiling, but he backed away. 'I'll see you at the church. Um—your make-up might need a little attention.'

'And you need a clean shirt,' she pointed out, laughing a little unsteadily, then Amy pulled her back inside, pushed him out and closed the door.

They were married at twelve, in the little chapel at Ashenden, in a simple, joyful ceremony attended by their closest family and friends, and one year later, they were back there for the christening of their son.

They called him Edward, in memory of the cousin

who had lost his fight against DMD just three weeks
before, and William, for his uncle.

Amy and Will and Chris Turner were his godparents,
and during the ceremony Sally rocked and shushed their
baby Lucie—Lucie, whose birth had shocked Will into
common sense, at last, and made him sell his horse and
stop taking foolish risks.

It was a beautiful day, and afterwards they took a picnic
down to the folly and drank champagne to celebrate.

There was so much to celebrate, so much to be thankful
for, and as they strolled back to the house that would eventually be their home, their baby sleeping peacefully in his
father's arms, Libby's heart was filled with joy.

'Happy?' Andrew asked, smiling down at her, and she
smiled back, her love flowing over.

'Happy,' she murmured. 'Very, very happy.'